MOA

by

Tricia Stewart Shiu

Illustrations and Cover Photo
by Sydney Shiu

MOA
by Tricia Stewart Shiu
Illustrations and Cover Photo by Sydney Shiu

Copyright © 2012 Human Being Publishing

ISBN: 0984002006
ISBN-9780984002009

Acknowledgments

To my daughter, Sydney: Thank you for sharing your gifts through the beautiful illustrations and cover photo. It is such a pleasure to collaborate with someone I love and admire. I appreciate you receiving my gifts, as well. Also, thank you to my insightful, clear, clever editor, Rebecca Gummere. What a joy it was to be able to work with you. The fact that you are my aunt makes our work even more precious. And thank you to my husband, Eric, for helping me carve out time to write. I'm sure it was not easy and I am grateful for your support.

Table of Contents

"As above, so below."

~ Hermes

CHAPTER I

The First Word

Ritual: Protection
Oil: Base of Almond Oil – Frankincense, Ginger,
Juniper Berry
Incense: Dried Sage
Incantation: "I am at ease."

Find a place where you will not be interrupted. Light the sage and allow the smoke to drift into all the corners of the room. Place a small amount of oil on your finger and anoint your forehead, chest and base of your spine. This will ground you during your incantation.

Close your eyes and imagine a ring of fire surrounding you. No one may cross without your permission. Picture a person, entity, situation for which you desire protection. See them approaching you within your circle of fire. Notice the feelings that arise. Express those feelings in any way necessary: scream, howl, yell at the person, cry...Now watch as the issue from which you desire protection attempts to enter the circle of fire. When they touch the fire, they are burned. They can come no further. Watch as they try again and again and, finally watch as they stop, move away and go home.

You are safe. Breathe in the safety, peace. Know that you are surrounded by protection.

✠

Eighteen-year-old Hillary Hause's left thumb searches frantically to turn on the "I'm Okay to Fly" hypnotherapy recording. Her nerves on edge, fuchsia fingernails press into the blue pleather armrests of her airplane seat.

"No spells can help you now," she whispers to herself under her breath—then checks to see if anyone notices. Nope, they don't.

The plane lifts through the early morning, gray fog of California, "June Gloom" giving way to the azure sky, and Hillary covers her curly brown head and retreats beneath the questionably clean plane blanket cranking the volume to drown out the drone of the engines.

"Outer shell close to breaking." This time she doesn't care if anyone hears.

I hover just beyond her "outer shell"—a movement in the periphery, a faintly familiar scent, a fond memory just beyond recognition, a non-human observer. Before the week is up, Hillary will save my life, as I will hers. But, for now, more about Hillary.

The drink cart rolls past the blanket, which has, by now, become a moist steamy cave.

"Hey, freak. I hope your plane crashes." The memory reverberates through her brain despite her attempts to distract herself with the hypnotherapy recording. She increases the volume, but the ugly conversation, which occurred just before school ended, still haunts her mind.

"I guess the only people they check on those flights are the suspicious ones," Krystal Sykes, a bully from her home room leans in as Hillary hastens to grab books for her next class. Krystal, also a senior, has hounded Hillary since the first day of freshman year and this is the final day during the final hour at this tiny high school of 376 students — where everyone knows everyone else's business.

"Look, Krystal." Hillary turns her eyes toward the sneering blonde. "It's the last day of school, we'll never see each other again. Can you give it a rest?" These are the most words the two young women have exchanged in the entire four years of high school.

A look of shock replaces Krystal's smug grin, "Oh, so now you talk." She leans in, so close that her spray tan becomes a patchy Impressionist painting. Her pores are blotched with cakey, two shades too dark powder, her unblended cream eyeshadow creases across the center of her lid and her tropical breeze flavored breath threatens to strangle the words right out of Hillary. "I know all about your witchcraft practices and have made a few spells of my own. Trust me. You'll never make it to your sister's house in Hawaii." Krystal's backpack jingles and Hillary watches her spin around and skip down the hall.

Hillary is not a witch. She has, however, carefully crafted a "shell" to protect herself from bullies like Krystal—who, as far as Hillary can tell, is not a witch either. She has watched Krystal throughout elementary, middle and high

3

school and has not been able to discern whether or not she practices witchcraft. No matter what Krystal's background, her intent is to harm. And there is nothing worse than a spell with an aim to hurt. Hillary has had no choice but to remain in a constant state of defensiveness.

The twenty-minute recording ends and Hillary falls into a troubled sleep—feeling every bump and hearing every creak of the plane.

With about an hour left in the flight, Hillary awakens with a "turtle headache." Hillary's older sister Molly taught her this term which means a headache caused by sleeping too long underneath the covers of one's bed.

Sadly, Molly lost her husband, Steve, last year in an unfortunate surfing accident. The throbbing pain in Hillary's left temple could be the result of remaining submerged beneath an airplane blanket and wedged between the window and armrest, or it could be from worry about how Molly and her niece, Heidi, are dealing with their devastating loss.

Disoriented, Hillary pokes her head out just in time to glimpse puffy clouds and sparkling sea below. A flood of excitement and sheer wonder flows through Hillary in the form of a tingle from her head to her toes. And then, a lovely thought: "...And for an Everlasting Roof, The Gambrels of the Sky..." She will enjoy this plane ride, thanks in part to Emily Dickinson.

It is then, that Hillary sees the shirt. From a certain angle, head leaning against the window, she can see between the window seats all the way to the first row. The shirt is bright orange with purple and green stripes and quarter-sized smiley faces running down the sleeve. Suddenly, the smiley faces animate. One frowns, another's mouth turns wavy. Mesmerized, Hillary watches as the stripes blink bright orange, purple and green. Then, she jumps as one smiley

4

face stretches over the back of the arm, its dotted eyes growing large and an outlined tongue darts out of its mouth. Did that smiley face just stick its tongue out at her? Covering her eyes with the blanket, Hillary slowly peeks one eye out of her self-made cover. Much to her relief, the shirt is no longer animated.

She needs some rest! Settling again, she tries to breathe deeply, imagining herself on a sunlit beach. But her attention is, again, drawn to the shirt. Who would wear such a shirt? And, more importantly, does it mean anything? Hillary cranes her neck over the seats and but cannot get up to go the bathroom because the plane's "Fasten Seatbelt" sign is lit. The only clue to the wearer's identity is his arm and his large hand with hairy knuckles. Maybe, she reasons, her temporary "experience" of seeing this animated shirt is a symptom of her tremendous fear of flying. Or, perhaps, this is a sign that she'll be okay.

For the time being, she chooses to interpret her reaction to the shirt as a good omen. Perhaps Krystal's misguided and potentially dangerous attempt at using witchcraft has failed. Also, her left elbow itches, another sign that good will prevail over evil...at least for today.

For the duration of the ride, Hillary occupies herself with figuring out who would wear such a ridiculously awesome shirt. Her fascination with anyone who dares to be different began during her first year in high school. Instead of buckling from social pressure, or changing into a homogenized clone, she chose to seek out other students who were relegated to the land of misfits. That land felt more like home to her than the fake smiles and fashion-obsessed antics of Krystal and her purposefully mean friends. Hillary found comfort in the sideways glances during lunch period or a knowing nod from a downtrodden classmate at her locker. They all stuck together even in their separateness. The land of misfits made her understand that being different doesn't have to be painful all the time.

The pilot announces the flight's end and Hillary turns her thoughts to the visit ahead. The gorgeous Hawaiian Islands are spread out like moss covered jewels in a magical, glittering sea. It isn't until the plane lands that she realizes she didn't have to use her hypnotherapy recording a second time.

When the gentleman with the unusual shirt rises to get his bags, there is nothing about him to distinguish him from a thousand other men. Medium build, stocky limbs and, well…that crazy shirt.

Then it happens again. The smiley face's tongue juts out, little drawn dots of spittle spraying from its lined mouth. There is no mistaking the shirt's animation this time. Hillary looks around to see if anyone else sees it too, but no one gives any indication that they've seen anything out of the ordinary. A second glance reveals the plain shirt, normal bright yellow happy faces in a smiley row. Hillary catches the man's eye and gives him a friendly nod. He returns her courtesy with a sour look of distain. Not at all the look she imagined the garment's owner would have had.

Perplexed at her mistaken interpretation of a "sign,"— she was sure that itchy elbow meant a friendly adventure was near—she is thrilled to be on solid ground. Hillary disembarks and immediately feels at peace. Although she is not a well-seasoned traveler—she has only been to Paris for a month during a student exchange—Hawaii is her favorite place to visit. And despite her distaste for flying, this place is absolute heaven—and therefore, worth the trip. Hillary has been visiting Honolulu since she was twelve years old, and even though her last visit was four years ago, the airport looks exactly like it did her first visit.

There are thatch-roofed kiosks selling plastic tiki statues peppering the baggage claim area. Bored muumuu clad women read romance novels next to racks of deep brown kukui leis and stacked boxes containing cans of roasted macadamia nuts. She meanders past the long narrow row of shops carrying everything from travel-sized mouthwash to mini chocolate Buddhas—leaving her in a religious etiquette quandary: to eat an awakened one or admire it from afar. The antiquated airport even smells like a vacation— fresh sea air mixes with jet fuel, auto exhaust and body odor—a whiff of freedom in a paradoxical cultural clichéd time warp.

Ukulele music escorts Hillary to a nearby glass display case with the words, "The History of Hawaii" sewn on a beautiful, dingy quilt. In front of the sign are two green-haired troll dolls dressed in grass skirts and coconut bras. The dolls are surrounded by tourist booty—boxes of chocolate caramel turtles, cans of macadamia nuts coated in everything from chocolate to garlic, and flavored kona coffee.

There is no turnstile for baggage. Luggage is simply placed on the floor in lines reminiscent of a life-sized domino game. She identifies her borrowed blue suitcase and exits.

The moist mid-afternoon heat clings to her shirt as she pulls her bags to the curb and waits for her sister Molly. Flurries of luggage-laden travelers scoot in and out of the sliding doors. Her sister's impeccably maintained tan four door SUV slips into an open space right in front of Hillary, and Molly hops out to help with the bags and give her younger sister a bear hug.

With much effort, the two heave Hillary's large suitcase into the hatch. Hillary throws her carryon in the passenger's seat and scoots in the back seat next to her cherubic seven-year-old niece, Heidi.

"Welcome to Hawaii, Auntie Hillary!" Heidi is nestled in her booster seat and leans toward her for a kiss on the cheek and squeeze.

"Thanks, Heidi." Hillary takes in her niece's unusual and beautiful ensemble—bright green leggings and one of Molly's purple, pink and yellow flowered silk wrap skirts fashioned into a unique child's sarong. Heidi's hair is pulled back into a high bun that is wrapped in a sequined snood, and Hillary's heart is flooded with a rush of love. She hugs Heidi again, and asks, "How is school?"

"Great! I'm going to be in second grade!" They hold hands for the rest of the ride. Hillary loves spending time with Heidi. The feeling is mutual. Hillary is only eleven years older than Heidi—almost the same age difference as she and Molly.

There is a surprising amount of traffic for noon on a weekday. Hillary gazes out the window then says absently, "How you doing, Mol?

Molly yawns, "We had a tough night last night."

No doubt, both she and Heidi have had quite a few sleepless nights since they lost Steve. Hillary can only imagine how difficult it has been for them.

The car rounds the corner to her sister's house, a gorgeous Victorian mansion. The front of the house has a portico of Corinthian columns through which is the entrance to the expansive ground floor. An enormous veranda filled with wicker rockers and love seats beckons to Hillary. As she walks in the front door, she imagines long ago times with men in linen suits and women in filmy dresses contentedly sipped iced tea. Steve's family has owned this house for more than 100 years. His paternal great-great-grandfather was a diplomatic advisor to King Kamehameha III, the third king of Hawaii who was famously known for the length of his reign: 29 years and 192 days—the longest in Hawaiian history—and his incredibly long name Keaweawe'ula Kiwala'o Kauikeaouli Kaleiopapa Kalani Waiakua Kalanikau Iokikilo Kiwala'o i ke kapu Kamehameha.

Heidi links arms with Hillary and the two skip up the concrete steps to the lovely open porch. This type of house is coveted on the island for its large plot of land and gorgeous lanai.

Heidi runs ahead of Hillary, up the wide oak staircase and yells, "You're staying up here, next to me, Aunt Hillary. Come on!"

If only she could bottle that energy! When Hillary finally reaches her cozy and bright room she keels over on the hand-sewn Hawaiian quilt. The decor, blue and green hues, creates a homey feel and is instantly comforting.

After a half hour rest, Hillary rises, and unpacks. Then, she changes into a long verdant patterned muumuu, smoothes on some coconut lip gloss—it makes her feel a part of the island—and peeks into Molly's room. Both she and Heidi are sacked out on Molly's four-poster mahogany bed. Hillary glides down into the enormous plantation kitchen. Steve's surf shop had done especially well and he and Molly had splurged on a kitchen redo.

She runs her hand over the old butcher-block, which has been sanded and refinished, as have the cabinets. This, along with the new stainless steel appliances, gives the entire kitchen a fresh updated look.

Pictures of Steve and the family still hang in a breakfast nook flanked by windows. One picture catches Hillary's eye. The family poses in front of Steve's surfboard. A four-year-old Heidi holds his hand on one side and Molly leans in with her head on his shoulder. Below this picture is one of Heidi's framed portraits of Steve. She's written the words "I love you, daddy." The warmth of this moment breaks Hillary's heart.

As much as she tries to push it away, a memory seeps into Hillary's brain. Steve's funeral was on the beach. The nearly one hundred people in attendance took turns sharing memories of their beloved friend, son, uncle, husband and father. When it was Heidi's turn, she looked intensely into the group and said, "I didn't get to say goodbye."

To break the sadness, Hillary steps out onto the lanai. Steve had told her that fifty plus years ago, this estate was surrounded by a quiet neighborhood. Now, streets and sidewalks abut the home. People and cars move quickly to important destinations, punctuating frustrations with a honk or two. At the end of the block, Hillary sees a park. Her memory slips again, this time to her final encounter with Steve. Molly, Heidi, Hillary and Steve had walked to Thomas Square Park, and he played tour guide to the family as they meandered around this beautiful state treasure.

Without another thought, Hillary runs back into the kitchen, grabs her purse and scurries to the park. It feels as if Steve is on her heels, about to explain the extreme mystical power the park holds, including the enormous and mysterious banyan trees.

CHAPTER II

Thomas Square Park

Ritual: Inner Voice

Oil: Base of Avocado oil—Marjoram Black Pepper, Nutmeg

Incense: Sweet Grass

Incantation: "Quiet my mind, open my heart."

Sit in a park or other public place. Light the sweet grass—make sure you are in an open area with no fire restrictions—walk in a circle allowing the smoke to create an invisible barrier. Anoint your throat and the back of your neck with the oil.

Close your eyes and imagine a light shining in your throat chakra. Speak the incantation aloud and as you do so, imagine that the words extend from you out into the world in rich blue energetic ribbons. These ribbons flow from you easily as you continue to say the incantation. Release these ribbons easily and freely out into the world.

You are heard. Breathe in love. Know that
your words are received with love and respect.

✦

As Hillary enters the stone archway of Sir Thomas Square Park, she can almost hear Steve's voice explaining the historical significance of the park. However, Hillary is gravely disappointed as she meanders around the grounds. This glorious shimmering gem is a mere shadow of what it was. She can't decide whether Steve's magical stories were so intense that they erased her memory of urban clutter or if the park has gone downhill at lightening speed. She sits on a wall next to an overflowing trashcan. Candy bar wrappers tumble over the bronze plaque bearing the name, "Sir Thomas Square."

Steve's warm voice echoes in her memory. "In 1843, Lord George Paulet overtook the Kingdom of Hawaii and declared the Islands to be under British rule. When Queen Victoria heard of the incredible miscarriage of justice, she immediately dispatched Admiral Richard Darton Thomas to reinstate King Kahmehameha III as sovereign ruler of Hawaii. This incident was known as the 'Paulet Affair.'"

"Lord George Paulet fled the island and was never heard from again. But some people believe he returned to England. Others say he had accomplices who helped him remain within the islands, hidden away. But I say..." at this point Steve lowers his voice to a whisper, "that Lord Paulet built a small shelter within a banyan tree pocket." Then with a leap forward Steve yells, "Look, there he is right now!" Hillary, Heidi and Molly squeal with fright, then—along with Steve—they all fall over in peels of laughter.

Hillary wanders over to a large bronze plaque, dusts off some grass clippings and reads:

This site was once a revered historical public ceremonial gathering place. On July 31, 1843 a celebration was held on behalf of Admiral Thomas during which this park was named in his honor.

Hillary tries to imagine the regal ceremony that was held beneath these incredible arbors. In bygone times, the stacked stone walls would have teemed with bountiful baskets of fruits, leis, hand-carved statuettes. She can almost hear the snap of hand-sewn flags fluttering in the strong tropical breeze. An enormous banyan tree covers the park and is surrounded by several other varieties of banyans as well as flowering shower trees. Among them is a rare variety of Hawaiian tree called "fish poison." Steve had described how, long-ago, fisherman would crush the tree's leaves and use the potent mash to stun fish so they would float to the water's surface, making them easier to catch.

Hillary smiles as she pictures Steve standing atop the low stone wall acting out the role of Hawaii's famous king. "Grateful to have sovereignty restored, King Kahmehameha turned to the breathless crowd," Steve raised his arms pretending to address his imaginary audience, "Ua mau ke ea o ka aina i ka pono," which means, "The life of the land is restored in righteousness. These immortal words have become the official motto of the State of Hawaii."

A paved stone patio is in the shape of the British flag and in the center is a fountain, its once sparkling 20 foot spout now a thick, murky green. Plastic bottles and cigarette wrappers float in the pool below.

I sit perched high atop the circle of banyan trees in Thomas Square. The traffic whirs just below and I watch Hillary dig through her large green leather purse. Rummaging through the mass of papers and essential oils, she unearths: a medium crystal ball, a large bundle of sage,

15

a cigarette lighter, a delicate and carefully crafted magic wand with crystal ends, a small sealed proprietary essential oil blend and a large leather bound diary.

The wand catches my interest and I zoom in for a closer look. Hillary's attention to detail is admirable. The handle has been whittled from oak and wrapped in a beautiful red and silver brocade fabric with gold edging. Semi-precious stones, the kind for divining powerful magic, adorn Hillary's enchanting, mystical tool. It has been fashioned out of clear quartz crystals to amplify, focus or transform any thought—good or bad—amethyst, to protect against witchcraft and rose quartz, to increase self-worth, inner peace and love.

Hillary has created her own brand of magic using crystals, personally crafted oils and rituals. Her small town branded her a witch in elementary school when her "Waterspout in a Box" presentation had an unusual outcome. An actual waterspout hit the town sending science fair participants and their families running for cover. No one was harmed, but this ill-timed occurrence started the magical ball rolling.

Even though Hillary knew she had nothing to do with the errant gale, people began to blame her in connection with all kinds of unusual events. One time a hawk burst through her school's assembly just as the principal was relating the strict "no tank top" rule. All eyes were on her—it was then that she realized she had been given a powerful tool—Assumed Power. For a while she reveled in watching people scramble as she walked into parties or down the hall at school. But then the invitations stopped and people just plain avoided her—which hurt more than the unnecessary brand of "witch." By high school, Hillary had been given a wide berth for so long that she just went with her social persona. If her classmates and their parents, which made

16

up most of the town, believed she had magic powers then so be it.

One event showed Hillary that, although not a witch, she definitely possessed special gifts. It was the height of the tourist season and—as usually happened during that time—a caravan of tour buses pulled up in the tiny town square. The locals dubbed these bi annual events the "Invasion." The first invasion occurred during the town's annual bell ringing ceremony in January to commemorate the Mission's first mass and the second was at the peak of the summer, in August, when the heat made the circular drive of cobble stones surrounding the town's show piece Mission and its glittering fountain radiate heat and spit steam as the cool water splashed over the adobe sides. Because their sleepy town was two hours away from the more popular tourist destination of San Clemente, Los Tardos rarely had visitors at any other time of the year.

Hillary would wander into town and sit, undetected near the Mission's side entrance. It was the perfect observation post because it was shaded and, in summer, nearly hidden from view by the full leaves of an oak tree. On this particular day, as she sat peering out from her protected hideaway, she found herself fascinated by a beautiful young girl close to her own age, dressed in a historical embroidered and beaded blouse with a matching skirt sitting on the edge of the fountain. Often girls in the town would dress the part, usually to sell food or drinks. The girl spoke to no one, her silky long hair nearly falling into the water, her elegant fingers rescuing the strands in the nick of time and tucking them behind her delicate ears. Periodically, she would look around at the wandering tourists, but not a soul spoke to her. The girl didn't move and neither did Hillary. They sat for hours this way.

Suddenly, the girl looked up and stared straight at Hillary and gave her a smile, but didn't move. Then, she slowly turned back to the water with a pleasant smile. Hillary was so shocked to be seen, she stayed put for a little longer. Finally, the crowd had dwindled down to just the two of them. When her curiosity was at its limit, Hillary finally came out of her shelter and approached the girl. Although they'd never met, Hillary felt that she'd seen this girl before.

"Hello," Hillary said with a smile. "You must not have sold much..."

Before she could finish her sentence, the girl vanished into thin air. Hillary's heart raced and she ran to the spot where the girl had sat for so long. It felt hot, as if the sun had been beating on it all day long. Without warning, Hillary felt incredibly thirsty and walked across the empty court-yard, through the open doors of the mission's vestibule to a drinking fountain and drank heartily. She had forgotten to bring water and was grateful that the hall was still open. After drinking her fill, she wiped her mouth with the back of her sleeve and turned to head outside. But what she saw stopped her in her tracks. Above the doorway into the vesti-bule was a large painted portrait of the girl she had seen at the fountain. Hillary's heart dropped to her stomach as she slowly stepped toward the plaque below the portrait. She read it aloud:

Senorita Matilde Regnetto (1812-1827) In honor of her self sac-rifice and service to the beloved Mission during her short time on earth.

"She was just 15." Hillary could not breathe.

She ran out of the Mission, through the vacant town square, the sun was sinking lower into the hills. When she arrived home, breathless, she pulled down a tome from her father's collection of Los Tardos history books. Funny, how Hillary never cared much for her father's curiosity about her small town's history, but suddenly she was desperate to know about Senorita Matilde Regnetto. And her questions were answered in an entire chapter devoted to this amazing young woman. She had never in her life had such an experience and desperately needed answers. The book detailed the senorita's childhood as tumultuous. Her father. Donato, was Italian and her mother, Marguerita, had been a Spanish clothes maker. The family of twelve settled in to Los Tardos in the mid-1800s and in 1819, six of the Regnetto children were turned over to the Mission's nuns for care after Donato abandoned the family and returned to his native Italy. Marguerita contracted tuberculosis and the nuns offered clean beds and meals in exchange for the children's work in the church.

Matilde was the oldest of the six children and considered herself their surrogate mother. During the August heat, a fire broke out in one of the Mission's anterooms and everyone managed to escape except the youngest Regnetto, Maria. Matilde pushed her way back into the raging fire, snatched Maria just before the heavy beamed ceiling collapsed and the two slipped out through a window to safety. Maria survived the massive blaze, but Matilde suffered from smoke inhalation, was badly burned and died three days later. The entire town mourned the loss of this brave young woman. A month later her mother died of a broken heart.

Hillary began to read every book she could find on the occult, past lives and mediumship. She was driven to know why she had seen Matilde and was convinced that this was a special gift. Now, she no longer felt like a fraud pretending to be someone or something she wasn't. With a newfound confidence she pursued her fascination with essential oils, crystals—and soon these other-worldly dalliances became a preoccupation. Finally, Hillary saw a way out of her social ills. Her knowledge of the occult was no longer merely a respite from the daily harassment of Krystal Sykes, Darla Melbert and Brenda Stone the "Threatening Three." The "Threats" made it their mission to create discomfort and fear wherever they roamed. Now, she saw a way to maintain control over her own protection. Hillary's "recipes" and magical rituals were, indeed, the best way to combat the "Threats" and anyone else who might try to harm her or her friends.

Just as Hillary is intrigued by the "magical world" I am truly captivated by the human world. Emotions and sensations abound in the human world, each person creating her own beautiful and unique concoction stirring up happiness or stirring up sadness. Fascinating!

Now more about me. My name is Moaahuulikkiaaakea'o Haanaapeekuluueehuehakipuunahe'e—Moa for short. Some call me a guardian angel, but I am far from anything of the sort. I am an Ancient Gatekeeper. In essence, I escort souls who have passed on through the Ancient Portal to the Light. The Ancient Portal is how I access my home and how other entities return to their own energetic source.

My form, for those humans who are willing to see me, is that of a dark-haired, seven year old girl. My clothing is simple. I wear only a soft, textured tan cloth or kapa, woven from the wauke bush. The kapa is wrapped around my chest and tied at the waist with a braided bark belt. I own no shoes, as I do not require them. I'm filmy or see-through when I show up on earth. That is because I can move and flow expanding or contracting my energetic mass into whichever place, in time and space, I wish to travel. This ability allows me to move about the city, through homes and even flow through people.

I spend most of my time floating above hotel cabstands or the U.S.S. Arizona Monument observing the unusual if not entertainingly predictable behavior of human beings.

My reason for watching Hillary is beyond entertainment value. She holds the fate of my very existence in her unaware hands. In three days, if she does not intervene, all of the Hawaiian Islands, including my home will cease to exist. This means that not only will my access to the Light be eradicated, but all access to the Light—anywhere on earth—will disappear. The Light will remain along with all the people who currently reside within Her immediate embrace, but no one else will ever again gain entry.

Hillary is blissfully unaware of me or of the adventure that awaits her. However, I happen to know she has been desperately longing for celestial contact. I am aware she never found the answers she sought with regard her fountain-side encounter with Matilde Regnetto.

Standing in the park, Hillary anoints herself with the oil on her forehead, inside of both wrists and the front of her chest, then flips through her well-worn diary, scanning the words. When she finds what she is looking for, with great certainty and flourish, Hillary begins to intone:

Breathe in life,
Breathe out death.
Bring the one who heals the breadth.
Open up eternal skies.
For those who mourn no last goodbyes.

A strong breeze shakes the underside of the banyans with a force that knocks over the vials of oil and sends her purse flying. As she stoops to gather the magical mess, the wind blows a crumpled paper smack into Hillary's face and it is instantly glued in place by her lip-gloss. Peeling the sheet away from her mouth, she smoothes the paper and is shocked to read the unmistakable words sloppily scrawled in dried mud across the center of the page:

21

Go Home!

During such a rituals, it is customary for the practitioner to take any unusual events seriously. Hence, she knows this message is meant for her.

Hillary hastily grabs the crystal ball, closes her eyes and breathes deeply then holds the ball up to a shard of sun just above her that pierces through the banyan leaves. The result is a strong glow around the shining globe and Hillary's hands. Suddenly, she feels a tremendous rush of anger. During the course of her magical practice, she has learned that when intense feelings come from out of the blue, most of the time, the emotions are not hers, but from someone else. Sometimes when people have strong feelings, they flow outside of their bodies and Hillary picks them up. Her empathic sensitivity in sensing others' emotions is included in some of her earliest childhood memories.

This particular feeling of anger hits powerfully, with no connection to her day so far. She's learned that since these emotions aren't her own, she can release them through rituals. "Blessed Goddess, I ask for your help in protecting Molly, Heidi and me. Please help me find the author of this note and release him or her from the karmic burden of anger. I ask for a sign that my prayers have been answered."

She sits and waits in self-monitored silence for her sign.

The beautiful Hawaiian morning breeze blows through the dangling tendrils of this ancient behemoth banyan on which I sit until the quiet is shredded by the blast of a taxi horn.

BEEEEEEEP!!

Hillary is jolted from her meditation by this jarring noise, her mid-length brown curls shuddering around her like a heavy lion's mane. She takes this aural interruption as a sign of completion and acknowledgment and begins to collect the aforementioned items and distribute them back

22

into her abyss of a purse. Her home, Los Tardos, California feels far away from the Honolulu hubbub. How in the world does Molly manage with a city this size?

Hillary's thoughts shift to Molly. The ten year age difference was difficult for them growing up, exacerbating just about every sibling issue that arose between the two. When Molly was eighteen, eight year old Hillary so desperately wanted her sister's attention that she would seek out ways to become injured when Molly was with her friends. In one incident, Hillary nearly fell off a balcony while trying to create the "best fort ever" for she, Molly and her friends. From then on, their relationship became a cat and mouse game—an endless chase. Hillary was the self-appointed ambassador of sisterly "fun" and Molly tried to ignore and evade any form of Hillary's entertainment which usually included frightful insects, tug of war and—her least favorite—punch buggy. I've witnessed Molly flinch when she sees a Volkswagen, just from the memory of Hillary yelling "Punch Buggy!" at the top of her lungs and slugging her in the tricep.

Hillary's penchant for all things "occult" has been a sore spot with Molly, who considers herself the voice of reason in the sisters' relationship. Unfortunately for Steve, he had the unenviable job of serving as the buffer between the two. He had been trained as a Shaman—a spiritual communicator and healer—and grew up with Huna—Hawaiian Mysticism—in his family, so he was no stranger to mystery. But even he had a tough time when Molly demanded physical proof of an otherworldly occurrence.

Despite her older sister's disapproval, Hillary continued her mystical practice. Her daily rituals grew out of a desperate need to protect not only herself from the "Threatening Three," but her entire school. Krystal, the head of the "Threats," had an affinity for pointed nasty barbs which were so accurate even teachers ran the other way when Krystal approached. However, Hillary's rituals were never meant to harm anyone, just to nudge any or all of the "Threats," including Krystal, away.

Hillary's friends Heather Gates and Shelby Hope banded together and dubbed themselves the "Three Mushketeers" or "Mush." The name was born from the threesome's fear of having their dignity pulverized, and their gatherings were less out of a desire for a connection to one another, but more to seek shelter from the social storm.

The "Threats" had three members and had been friends with the "Mush" in Middle School, but Darla and Krystal began to write letters to Hillary, Heather and Shelby under the guise of fashion and behavioral support and offered the enticement of opening the doorway to popularity. This is when Darla and Krystal found Brenda and became a Greek Chorus-like trio commenting on Hillary's wardrobe, picking apart her choice in haircut and imposing their special brand of "help." One particular ritual centered on a mean note addressed to the Mushketeers expressing distaste for each girl's dress, personal hygiene and existence at school. So jarring was this letter, Hillary arranged a "Circle" with the "Mush" in her family's backyard. She formulated a ritual meant to move the "Threats" focus away from "The Mush" and back to something a little more constructive, like schoolwork.

She built a small fire in her family's charcoal barbecue with sticks she'd gathered from a large oak tree and bundled them with red ribbon. On the top of the bundle, she placed a wad of newspaper, lit it and watched the paper absorb the fire and then catch the sticks within its increasing glow. Heather and Shelby entered the backyard, stood close to Hillary and watched the flames hiss and swirl above the container. During the ritual, Hillary encouraged the "Mush" to throw items in to the fire to release or express fearful emotions out of their bodies and into the fire. Heather had, unbeknownst to Hillary, made a Voodoo doll—complete with real hair cultivated from a purloined brush and scraps of fabric from Krystal. The circle took on an eerie feel as Heather came forward with the doll and threw it into the fire with an uncharacteristic cackle. For a moment, Hillary half expected to see the smoke curl into a skull and crossbones like some evil cartoon, but the fire continued to spark and crack normally. Then a loud explosion within the fire sent the doll hurling straight through the air, over Hillary's house and into her neighbors yard. The group ran for cover, under a patio umbrella.

Hillary's stomach dropped. She had broken the cardinal rule of keeping kind intentions in her magical work and hissed at Heather, "What are you trying to do, kill us all?"

"S...sorry. I just can't stand Krystal." Heather burst into tears. "Now something awful is going to happen because of me."

Upon hearing the neighbor yell over the fence, "What the...Hey, what are you doing over there!" The girls ducked inside and found shelter in Hillary's room.

"You know," Shelby whispered. "Krystal has told me so many times that I should go take a flying leap. Looks like she did it tonight." Then she broke out into a big grin,

Heather calmed down and she giggled. "She really soared, didn't she?"

The "Mush" went home, laughing off the idea that Heather's act would result in any wrong. Hillary did her best to laugh it off, but fell into an uneasy sleep that night and dreamt she was being chased by a dragon.

The following day, when Krystal fainted in the hallway, Heather confessed to her parents in a panic, which created a chain reaction of epic proportions. Hillary's parents were sited by the City council for "Unlawful Use of Projectile Explosives." Apparently, Heather had used her brother's empty can of Silly String as the body for the Voodoo Doll. Not only was Hillary banned by her parents from creating any more such gatherings, now the city had banned her as well, sending her into a deep "research" phase. Never again did she include her friends in her "Circles." Essentially, Hillary went underground with her practice, feeling misunderstood and alone. Her own parents, although they loved her dearly—had no idea how to deal with Hillary's social issues. Molly had never been like this—she was voted "Most Popular," was head cheerleader and thanked her parents profusely during her Valedictorian speech at graduation. Therefore, they were shocked when Hillary turned down several dates to prom, began working at an occult bookstore and dyed her brown curls jet black.

Hillary has continued her self-made rituals and through study and research has developed a comforting—and I might add, more powerful than she knows—set of rites. The basis of her rituals was from a kind place with a motive to heal herself and those around her. Things could have been a lot worse for Hillary during her school years, had it not been for her steadfast commitment to create peace wherever she went. Her path became decidedly solitary, however, and Hillary began more and more to fear being "found out." If that happened, she knew would be expelled from school and likely shunned in her small, conservative town.

Because Molly was already out of the house during this phase, she wrote off the changes in Hillary's dress and demeanor as a Goth stage. Molly eschewed everything metaphysical and, instead, she has become fixated on the present—a staunch realist. Molly is striving to raise Heidi in her own image—to be independent and clear thinking.

Hillary's trip is courtesy of their parents—a warm couple who brought up their two daughters in sleepy little Los Tardos, a community of 12,000 residents located just outside of San Clemente. San Clemente, is a beautiful beach town nestled along the coast just north of San Diego. Los Tardos is known for its minuscule mission with a crumbling fountain, the repairs being voted down every term, as well as the annual sounding of the Los Tardos Mission bell. This year's ring will make it 130 years.

Hillary's mother knew nothing of metaphysics and believed that everything could be solved with a cup of warm milk and a firm hug. Her father applied a more hands on approach to Hillary's social woes. His angle for Hillary's bullying was self-defense. He taught her how to box and gave her a whistle for her fifteenth birthday. Even through their misguided stabs at supporting her, Hillary adored her parents. Until, that is, the day before she left for this glorious graduation trip to Hawaii.

The journey had been planned well before Molly's husband's tragic surfing accident. Although Hillary was hesitant to come, Molly insisted. Their father, believing that his daughter would be much better off if she faced her fear of flying without her hypnotherapy recording, took her iPod for safe keeping. Hillary discovered that the iPod was missing three hours before she left and tore the house up one side and down the other looking for it. Finally, she asked her mother who referred her to her father who proudly proclaimed that no daughter of his would have to rely on a schlocky, psuedo-science to get through a flight. She could do it on her own. He presented her with a carefully prepared bag including two packs of peppermint gum, a paper sack—in case of hyperventilation—a copy of the Magazine "Modern Teen" and a Snickers bar—to eat as a reward when she made it to the end.

Frustrated by the misunderstanding and fueled by fear of her impending flight, Hillary flew into a rage, demanding that he return her iPod immediately. Although her father was shocked by this unprecedented outburst, he found Hillary's anger funny and began to chide her—surely she could tough it out. In the end, he reasoned, she would thank him.

Those words broke the dam that held back every upset about being misunderstood during her high school years. After her rant, her father unearthed the missing iPod and tossed it at Hillary in disgust. No daughter of his should ever use hypothetical nonsense, like hypnotherapy, as a crutch.

To her own shock and horror, anger spewed from every part of her as Hillary screamed obscenities at her parents. She berated them for all of her loneliness and angst and said she would be out of the house as soon as her trip ended. With that, she stormed out of the house and took the city bus to the airport. As she lugged her heavy suitcase down the crowded gate, Hillary knew Molly would never have behaved like this.

Molly moved to Honolulu to marry Steve, and they had Heidi right away. Molly and Steve had been college sweethearts. Although their marriage wasn't perfect, they always managed to share laughter. Hillary loved listening to Steve's stories about growing up on the island, seeing ghosts and battling sharks. She'd sit at the breakfast table while he effortlessly wove tales and served up gargantuan stacks of buttery pancakes with guava syrup. Then he told her how to win when confronted by a shark. "Punch 'em in the nose," he said with a wink. She marveled at the rich family life they cultivated and basked in their warm and loving relationship.

Now that he's gone, Hillary sees the wear that the last year has put on Molly. Her once radiant face is sallow, her cheeks are sunken and there is a slight edge to her normally vibrant personality. Her default expression is blank and empty.

Hillary rises, stretches her lanky frame— the swelling traffic and noise level rouse her from her comfortable spot under the Thomas Square Park's banyan trees—then begins the slow walk back to Molly's house. However, upon her first step, she catches her foot on a long banyan tendril and falls onto a, thankfully, soft patch of earth. As she unhooks the tree's gangly limb from her shoe, a glint of light catches her eye. She brushes a large green leaf away and dusts off a quarter-sized stone. Its opalescent sheen glimmers in the diffused morning light. The stone doesn't resemble any of the typical island rocks Hillary has ever seen. Molly has told her a couple of stories of tourists who have taken volcanic rock or coral from the island with dire results—car crashes, mysterious illnesses and troubles that last long after a visitor has left the island. Funny that such superstition should come from such a skeptic.

Another breeze shoves a wayward limb into Hillary's back and she spies a sparkling pool on the ground in front of her, but as she moves to it, the pool of light disappears. She dusts off the multi-faceted stone, sticks it in her pocket—Hawaiian curses be damned—and heads off to meet her sister and niece for a hearty Hawaiian breakfast.

Imagine a world in which pain, confusion nor frustration exists. A loving warm light surrounds and embraces you, and a light family celebrates your very existence. Everyone has accepted herself, which brings all divine light into each and every interaction within this amazing world. This is my home. And that shimmering pool that Hillary so briefly saw? That was the final access to my home world, disappearing before her eyes as the celestial doorway slammed shut.

From now on, I must rely on Hillary, her sister and niece, who must confront their past to save my life and eventually, theirs. They will find they'll need every ounce of bravery and cunning they possess to help us move forward in our quest.

I drift within the circle of enormous banyan trees, and do my best to take solace in remembering that this day was destined to happen and that Hillary is the only one who has agreed to come to my aid, even though she does not yet remember her vow to me.

That evening, Hillary rests on the guest bed, arm over her head, quietly mumbling in her sleep. It is ten past midnight and I stand in front of her, ready to announce my presence.

"Hello. Hillary." I quietly say.

I've found that an air of mystery is the best way to create maximum impact. Hovering right above her bed and quietly asking for attention is the best way to approach someone who is new at acknowledging a light entity. Although, it is not necessary for me to do it this way, I feel it is important to shield Hillary's young psyche from what is about to unfold. Her youth, however, does not preclude her from power. Magic is just the tip of the iceberg. She possesses everything necessary to reopen the portal to my home. She is simply in need of training.

She stirs slightly then settles back into sleep but not before saying, "Wait! I've got frogs to seize and leaves to grout."

The trouble with humans, is even when they speak clearly, they're often incoherent. Hillary was chosen, because she was willing—at least in spirit—to participate with the Ancients and, therefore, me. Before Hillary was born, she was a ball of light. This is true of all humans. Each person begins his or her journey to life in the Universal light.

We met during our time in the Light and, in fact, made fast friends. It was then that she agreed to join forces with me. We made our pact before she was born, however as she grew, she forgot the agreement. Most humans forget the agreements that are made while they are in the Light. Either they are lost during birth or as a child assimilates into "normal" human life—school, friends, play—the memories of their glorious time in the Light are lost. Getting Hillary to wholeheartedly agree to join forces with someone she doesn't remember will be the hardest part. The next item on the list is still ahead; helping her move her awareness of her commitment to her conscious self. Even though she is open to otherworldly experiences, she may not understand or even agree to my current proposal.

Molly's house is about five miles from the ocean. So, instead of the roar of the waves that used to lull me to sleep, Hillary and I must settle for the gentle whoosh of the traffic below. This is a different Hawaii from my home of long ago. In my youth, I played on the shore, molded the sand into shapes and swam with sea turtles. Yes, I was once human.

CHAPTER III

Humanity

Ritual: Removal of Obstacles
Oil: Base of Kukui Oil – Geranium, Melissa, Clove
Incense: Sage
Incantation: "I see the light to my divine path."

Find a place where you will not be interrupted. Light the sage and sit while the smoke surrounds you. Anoint your third eye with the oil. See your biggest obstacle in front of you. Now, examine it from every angle. How big is it? What color? Shape? What feelings does it evoke? Then, it delivers a message. Your obstacle's job is done. Bid it farewell and watch it dissolve into a puddle and get absorbed by the earth where it will be recycled into love.

Freedom is yours. Breathe in love. Know that your divine path is acknowledged and you may proceed as planned.

A ship carrying strange men with long dark beards and brown faces stormed our shores first demanding food and drink, then grabbing anything of value from my family's dwelling. Father stubbornly refused and was killed along with my mother and two sisters. It happened so quickly, there was no time to cry. The marauders ransacked our house and stole a beautiful black coral carving of Ku, the god of prosperity and production. Mother was given the carving as payment for her diligent work on a kapa for a wealthy chief. She was revered as an expert weaver and created elaborate ceremonial, gorgeous, uniquely printed kapa bark cloths from the Wauke bush. Each morning we said a prayer to this delicate six-inch tall statue inlaid with precious pink coral. My blood boiled imagining our treasure in the filthy hands of such brutish men.

I fled for my life into the brush and hid among the thorny gorse bush spines. Crying and weakened from grief and terror, I prayed the Huna Prayer, asking for protection and salvation from my terrifying predicament. I began to breathe and gather Mana—vital life energy—and send it to my highest self as I'd been taught to do by my Popo—grandmother— years before. Our practice created a powerful bond with her and when she passed—a mere month before—I would feel her spirit around me during my daily practice. Oh, how I missed her! As I sat amidst thorns and breathed the Mana, something extraordinary occurred—my grandmother's spirit came to me and lit up a small glowing hole in the earth, just large enough for me to enter. I did so in great haste and was enveloped in a protective, warming white light.

Popo said that I'd entered the world of the Ancients and was safe. However, to continue to remain protected by the universal force, I had to agree to guide pre-selected humans through the portal to the Ancient world. Their own guides would meet them and take them to their destination of truth. Thus, I began my work as gatekeeper for the Ancient Portal.

I've transitioned many souls from their bodies through the portal—generations, in fact. My gift is to live between the worlds. And since my body did not die, but merely "transformed," I exist in a vibration accessible only to those humans who choose to believe in and acknowledge my presence.

It was initially human's freedom to choose whether or not to go through the Ancient Portal that balanced and stabilized earth. You see, humans are a part of the earth and its energetic ecosystem just as the plants and trees are a part of the earth's flora and fauna bionetwork. The lower emotions such as anger and hatred can cause this planet's energetic balance to shift. The less freedom or free will humans have, the easier it is for them to regress into a lower and more negative emotional state, thus creating barriers between the earth and the Ancient world. Because of this imbalance, the portals began closing and I was given the task of "gatekeeper," so to speak. Now I keep that balance in lieu of "free will and choice."

My true home is in the Ancient world. I've loved performing the essential duty of escorting souls from bodies to ensure their safe return to their destined spiritual repository. My task is essential to the survival of the Hawaiian Islands because, although humans die, their souls must be transferred to the appropriate location. If not, and too many souls remain within the islands energetic constructs, the earth's energy will become unbalanced causing natural disasters like volcanic eruptions and earthquakes. It is the human soul, which, upon transitioning to another state, balances and stabilizes the island energy. Now, sadly, the portal is closed, and as difficult as it is to accept the closing of all access to my home, I must remain focused on saving

Hawaii. For if I do this with Hillary's help, I have the best chance of re-opening the portal.

There are humans who assist my work. They are called Anuenue—pronounced Ah-Nooey-Nooey—and, although fully human, they possess a gift for communicating with the ancients. It is rare to encounter an Anuenue in person, for their work is energetic and usually done from afar. They walk on this earth experiencing life as humans and have the power to heal anything related to humans—health issues, relationship issues—however, they cannot heal the earth or energetically change it in any way. The word, Anuenue, means Rainbow, for no one but the rainbow truly knows the location of its end. Because of their inability to heal the earth, none of these highly mystical beings possess the power for opening the portal to the Ancient world.

Some of the Anuenue are angry because they do not want this "transitioning way" to change. Happiness for them is keeping their job, of "spiritual translator." Anuenue earn the right to become an energetic entity, like me, by ushering people through. For them, it's a numbers game. The more people they support in transitioning through the portal, the closer they are to immortality. I report to the Light Consortium, a Master Group of ancient souls who counsel entities like me. They cannot intervene in any issue, but may advise. The Anuenue report to me.

Watching Hillary sleep, I hover inside this smartly arranged room, undetectable. The household has been inhabited by kind and loving souls, both masters and servants. Most humans would think I'm a housefly. Hillary is uneasy with my presence even though she doesn't consciously acknowledge I'm here—and she rolls from side to side. But her discomfort with my presence lets me know she is aware, at least on an unconscious level, that I'm here. And although she doesn't see it yet, she's in for the adventure of a lifetime. If, that is, she accepts.

Here's another problem with humans—free will. Humans have the ability to choose and the pesky "universal law" wreaks havoc with my assignments. My assignment, with regard to Hillary, is simple—persuade her to help in saving the Ancients' access between the worlds.

Lord George Paulet penned the mysterious and worrisome note she found during her ritual, demanding that she leave the island. She has no idea that he is her great-great-great grandfather.

Lord Paulet is a "lost soul." After death, some souls remain in an unknowing state in which they, falsely, believe they are eternally alive. When this happens, they remain in a loop of consciousness and their unfinished business continues to play out over and over again.

After Admiral Thomas reestablished Hawaiian rule, Lord Paulet fled to another part of the island where he found and entered a portal transitioning through a similar process as I. He refused guidance on the other side and continues his fight to gain control of the Hawaiian Islands. However, since he is no longer a human, he is now fighting a battle of control over access to the island—via the portal. Life goes on without him, buildings are built and rulers come and go, however, in his mind, the Island is still his and he must try to capture it.

I've had enough of waiting for Hillary to wake up. I blow a cold gust of wind at her feet, exposing her tootsies to the evening air.

Nothing.

Molly softly snores in her sleep in the other room. She is dreaming of her late husband during happier times. I must remember to mention that Steve sends his regards. But now, on to more pressing items, asking Hillary for help.

This time, I whisper and send a chilly gust of air toward her head. "Hillary." My voice wafts through the air and does the trick.

Hillary sits bolt upright and pops one eye open, which stares mercilessly through me. Then, she falls sideways back onto the pillow eyes closed. Sometimes it takes people a few minutes to calibrate their vision to my presence. She groans, blinks, closes her eyes then opens one. Poor thing has never seen or experienced anything like me.

She closes her eyes and sleepily pulls the green cotton blanket over her head. But I know she's not asleep. She's wondering what woke her up—was it a noise, a dream?

I try again. "Hello, Hillary."

My voice is clear and open. She finally sees me! My form is that of a seven-year-old girl with sleek dark brown hair, curious and snapping hazel eyes. I draw myself up to my full height—four feet five inches—and smile as warmly as I can.

She does a quick check in and still feels her body on the air mattress and is aware of her surroundings, so she scrunches her eyes shut then pops one open.

"Um, hi." She thinks she's dreaming. Then she blurts, "Who are you?"

I proudly answer with my full Hawaiian birth name, "Moaahuulikkiaaakeee Haanaapeekuluueehuehakipuu..." and upon seeing her blank reaction, I add, "Just call me, Moa."

"Okay, Moa." She checks in with herself again and, believing she's asleep and decides to enjoy this interesting albeit highly vivid dream. "I'm listening."

"You invoked me. Remember?

Breathe in life,
Breathe out death.
Bring the one who heals the breadth.
Open up eternal skies.
For those who mourn no last goodbyes.

I'm 'the one who heals the breadth.' Steve is okay, by the way."

"Uh...Steve?" She rubs one eye and sits up a little straighter than before.

"He's busy fulfilling his ancestral destiny on the other side. Now...how would you like to save Hawaii?" Upon seeing the puzzled look on her face, I take a different tack, "You've been chosen to help heal your family and, in the process, save the Hawaiian islands."

Hillary's eyes are still open, but they glaze over with information overload.

"First thing you need to do," I continue, "is tell your sister that her husband says 'hi.' Even though his initial departure from earth was abrupt, he has transitioned nicely and sends his best wishes." Then, I add as an afterthought, "Oh, and I'll arrange it so that you'll run into an old friend of Molly's, Sharon, tomorrow when you're out on a walk. This will prove that what I say is true. Perhaps then you'll agree to help me with the Ancient portal?"

"Well...it's Moa, right?"

I nod encouragingly.

"You're...how old...five or six?"

"Well, I was seven when I became an Ancestral Gate-keeper..."

Hillary interrupts, "There are probably better games to play than this. Why don't you fly on down to Heidi's room?

I'm sure she'll be thrilled to have a visit from a local girl about her age."

With that, Hillary flips over and quickly falls back to sleep.

Okay, she asked for it.

CHAPTER IV

Hot! Hot!

Ritual: Invoke Ancient Wisdom
Oil: Base of Avocado Oil – Barberry, Lavender, Vetiver
Incense: Sage
Incantation: "Part the veil to reveal what I already know."

---

*On a Full Moon, gather three twigs. Clear yourself and the twigs
by running them through the smoke of the burning sage. Anoint
each twig with the oil as well as your third eye, throat, heart and
just below your belly button. Pick up the first twig and exhale your
intention to part the veil between you and the wisdom of your
lineage. Throw each twig into a fresh or salt-water source and say
the incantation as you do so.*
*Ancient wisdom is yours. Breathe in unconditional love. Know
that your words are received with love and respect.*

"**H**ot, hot, hot...hot!" Heidi cheerfully chants. She bounces and hops moving her arms and clapping like a cheerleader. The sun shimmers in her long, straight light brown hair and she sports an indigo tutu, pastel blue leggings with hearts and a yellow and fuchsia smiley face t-shirt. If she were a cartoon, birds and musical notes would trail her every step.

"Sure is." Hillary manages.

Even though it is only 10 o'clock, it's blazing. Molly's sleek, leggy frame slips slightly ahead of the trio, her auburn wavy hair trails after. Hillary pulls a rolling "snack bag," which is loaded with every snack known to womankind. She and Molly have taken turns pulling it—her sister insists that it is easier than each of them carrying heavy purses, sunblock and other travel necessities. The enormous bag bangs rhythmically against her right heel as she walks and the effort of hauling it causes sweat to pour from every part of her body and pool in her midsection. The result is a large trickle moving toward her undies—thank God she wore cotton.

Ah, telepathy and its frightening advantages. I stay far enough away, that neither Hillary—regardless of her pooling sweat—nor Heidi can detect my presence. Children are sensitive beings and have a much better energetic understanding of the world than adults. Let's say I'm nowhere and everywhere at the same time.

"Uh, Molly, do you think Heidi needs some water?" Hillary huffs, then mumbles, "I know I could use some."

"No thanks. Heidi's fine." Molly shouts behind then trots ahead as Hillary yanks the roller bag up a large ramp onto the searing sidewalk and makes little effort to hide her annoyance.

"We'll get some out of the snack bag once we're inside, Aunt Hillary." Heidi chirps. "You'll be fine."

The threesome walks toward the Blaisdell Convention Center, which is a few blocks down from Molly's house. Molly chose the Chinese Cultural Festival as an afternoon activity to inject a little culture into Heidi's sponge-like mind and escape the noonday sun. Heidi sings to herself as the two women cross the street and move onto the covered sidewalk. Molly directs the mini wagon-train around a blind corner to a large concrete ticket booth, then squeals, "Sharon!"

The women embrace. Sharon is wearing khaki shorts and a light blue linen shirt. Her medium length, layered, black hair is streaked with silver strands. But, Hillary's heart stops when she hears the name, and she is stunned to see Molly has begun to cry. Sharon gathers Molly in a close embrace, holding her as Molly tells her of her husband's untimely death.

"Hey, Aunt Hillary." She feels a tug on her arm, and Heidi stage-whispers, "Moa was right!" Then, as Hillary's brain spins at hearing Heidi speak my name, the child walks purposefully to Molly's side and threads her arm around her mother's slim waist.

Hillary stands dumbfounded, next to the Blaisdell Center ticket booth, sweating more now, with both heat and shock. She tries to maintain her composure as Molly introduces Sharon.

Sharon leans in and embraces Hillary. Cloves and strawberry perfume oil curl into Hillary's nostrils and she attempts to steady herself partly from this unusual scent and also from utter disbelief. The two step back and Heidi—arm still around Molly's waist—takes Hillary's hand.

"How long will you be in town, Hillary?" Sharon's calm manner draws Hillary close.

"A month." Hillary smiles and tries to match the warmth and kindness that is being extended.

"Can you come with us, Auntie Sharon?" Heidi asks hopefully.

"Sorry Hiwalani. I have to shop for my trip. But we will see each other when I return next month. Your mother and I will see to that." Sharon's closeness to Molly and Heidi is shown by her use of the Hawaiian term for beloved child. She leans down and hugs Heidi and kisses her on the forehead. "You be good for Makuahine. Molly, I'll call you when I return. And Hillary, so nice to meet you."

And as they walk away, Molly fills Hillary in on the details.

Right after Steve's death, Molly had tried to contact Sharon, an old friend of his family. When Molly moved with Steve to Honolulu, Sharon made sure she was included in every community activity from luncheons to fundraisers and within six months, she had more friends than she could count. But as Molly struggled to take care of Heidi, manage Steve's business affairs and pay the bills, she lost touch with many people, including Sharon. When Molly finally emerged from postgrief fog, she began to regain communications with her old friends. However, when she tried calling the clothing store in which Sharon worked part time, the clerk said she'd no longer worked there. Sharon had moved with no forwarding address and her email had changed. It was as if Sharon had vanished into thin air. Finally, Molly accepted that they might never meet again.

As the three wander through the endless stalls of the Cultural Center, Hilary attempts to casually extract information from her niece. "So, Heidi…You mentioned Moa. Where did you hear that name?"

"We met last night. She came by after she spoke with you and told me all about Sharon. Isn't she cool!"

A chill runs up Hillary's spine. "What else did she say?"

"That's all," Heidi skips ahead toward her mother, but not before calling behind her, "Oh, she said you should have asked before you took the shiny stone from Thomas Square."

Hillary stops dead, the buzz of people around her creates a soft cushion against the frightening clang inside her head.

When a thought pattern is broken, sometimes the "noise" within stops, but other times, it increases. This is what Hillary is experiencing—a shift in consciousness.

"C'mon, Auntie." Her niece shakes Hillary from her stupor, "Let's get some Shave Ice!"

The cool sweetness of the Shave Ice is just what Hillary needs to calm her newly awakened spirit.

Although hours have slipped by, the searing sun pulls the final bits of vivacious energy from Heidi. The group walks home in silence until they reach the coolness of the front foyer.

"Naptime!" Heidi announces.

Molly and Hillary nod in agreement and plod heavily up the solid stairs to bed. They'll all take a quick snooze before they will go to the market and choose some items for dinner. In the safety of her room, Hillary breathes quietly and deeply. She slips under the cool sheets with a sense of relief mixed with psychic exhaustion. I watch her eyelids flutter in response to her nervous system calming. She is almost asleep.

Mid afternoon is the best time for sleep. That is how it was when I was a small child. My mother would let us loll on a soft bed of leaves under the Wauke tree. This sacred plant gave us cloth for our ceremonies and bedding, its waterproof cover offering a safe dry place to rest during the rainy parts of the day. I would drift in and out of consciousness, imagining life as a grown woman creating kapa or cloth from the special tree. I'd pound out the Wauke's pithy insides, performing the ritual that many had before me—washing, pressing, rinsing, pounding—then proudly stamping my kapa cloth with my own watermark.

The unique branding of my kapa would come from my own choice of colors, binders and scents. Although some dyers used binders like salt/pa'aki, mud/lepo or even urine/mimi, I would dye my cloth a soft pinkish orange using a paste of crushed coral and sea water. Finally, my kapa would be scented with iliahi/sandalwood and stored for my first keiki's or child's arrival.

Sadly, I cannot show pass more family's lore to Hillary because, with the introduction of foreign fabrics, the Wauke is impossible to find.

This time Hillary speaks first. "Hi Moa."

She is asleep, but speaking to me from a twilight state—fully asleep, yet she feels completely awake. To her it feels like an ultra-real dream.

"Hello, Hillary."

"Okay. Who are you?" Hillary's heart feels like it is going to pound right out of her chest. After all, her rituals were focused on drawing in "otherworldly" beings, but now that I'm here, it is almost more than she can take. She scoots away, presses her back against the carved oak headboard, pulls the sheet up to her chin and awaits my response.

"I was born on Oahu during the first generation of Hawaiians and transitioned into an Ancient being. A portal exists, which allows access between the human world and the Ancient world. Your great-great-great-grandfather was part of the first groups of Spanish visitors to Oahu. With them, they brought a number of illnesses and disease, which caused thousands to die. Moreover, their presence imposed a belief system on the Hawaiian souls that restricted access to the portal. Before this, Hawaiians had unrestricted access. Through ritual, ancient Hawaiians were able to travel freely between the ancient world and earth."

Hillary looks bewildered, but alert.

"Now souls must be escorted to the other side. That is my job. The entrance has closed and you are the only one who can open it. The act of "Belief" is the first step in gaining access to the portal."

"Why me?" Hillary's body tenses.

"You agreed to this a long time ago—way before you were born. When you were in your Light body, you vowed that if the portal was ever in danger, you would sacrifice your mortal shell to defend its access."

47

"Wait. Sacrifice my mortal shell. That sounds like I might be killed."

"Perhaps...But I know Protection Protocols..."

"No way."

Hillary thrashes around and wakes herself up. That's the end of our conversation. Maybe it's best. She needs time to assimilate this new information.

And, although time expands and contracts in form in the ancient world—meaning 5 minutes could be 5 years, 50 years or even 5 seconds—I've gotten clear messages that point to a mere 72 hours left to save the Islands and restore access to the portal.

After that, the opening will self-seal and access will be eliminated forever. Then the true destruction will occur. Hundreds of underground volcanoes surrounding the Hawaiian Islands will erupt causing the water level to rise, which will submerge them completely under the Pacific Ocean.

The wind has picked up and lifts the palm leaves then carelessly drops them to fend for themselves in the next gust. My mode of travel ranges from image travel—sending my thoughts to a location, then my immaterial self follows, or sometimes I use the elements—air, water, fire or earth— to get from one place to another. I opt to take the air and fly on a long route through the dancing palm fronds. I am curious to return to the site of the portal and examine it more fully. The city buzzes along as I float slightly above the treetops. Shoppers meander, a surfer returns from the beach with surfboard sticking out of his sunroof. All are oblivious of the looming disaster.

The entrance to the Ancient World was first formed with the island of Oahu. In fact, there were many portals within each island. With time and neglect, however, Honolulu ended up being the only safe place left. Wars, illnesses and negativity all slowly dissolved the energetic constructs within each gateway. The requirement for maintaining each entrance is clear intent balanced with soft heart energy. Everyone is born with a loving heart, a soft heart. However, each soul's journey includes challenges in which humans must endure grief and loss, heartache and peril. Many humans allow these events to harden their hearts and create shells of resistance to any new experiences.

New experiences create positive healthy energy. The inhabitants of the Hawaiian Islands are in danger of suffering a terrible state if consciousness is not shifted toward a more positive and creative energetic stance. With the world continuing into a negative spiral, the Hawaiian Islands devastation will only be the first in a chain of disastrous events, which will eventually impact each and every land base on earth. Soon the entire world population will be in danger of extinction. Hillary's heart has hardened with her exposure to the "Threats" and the judgment of her small town, but her condition can be reversed. I will ensure that she will be surrounded by protection and love during this most arduous task. Our lives depend upon it.

CHAPTER V

The Other Side

Ritual: Luck
Oil: Base of Almond Oil – Thyme, Sage, Basil
Incense: Basil
Incantation: "Good begets good."

Choose a stone—any kind will do—and clear it by letting it sit overnight in the light of the new moon. Anytime thereafter, anoint the stone and your palms. Light the basil and let it burn while you perform this ritual. Hold the stone between your palms and say the incantation. Bury the stone next to a tree.

Believe you will receive your heart's desire in divine timing. Good begets good, so do something kind for someone else and it will return tenfold.

"Hey, Heidi. Do you want to do something fun?" Hillary kneels down next to her niece.

It is eleven thirty in the morning on a day which has dawned bright and clear. Molly, Heidi and Hillary have staked out a prime spot on the soft sand at Waikiki Beach. This is a favorite spot of both vacationers and locals because the waves are not as strong or large as the ones on the North Shore and it has accessibility to shops, restaurants and hotels. The clear water and expansive beach of Waikiki is perfect for beginning surfers, sunbathers and swimmers.

"Sure." Heidi sits up on her heels, dusts the sand from her hands and waits for instructions.

Hillary leans in, "We'll create a play circle. Let's collect 5 rocks. Any shape or size will do."

"Cool." Heidi spots a beautiful white stone. She holds up the rough porous stone about the size of her fist. "How's this?"

"Great! Keep going. By collecting the stones, we are gathering happiness and love to put in a circle of energy. Then we can send the happiness and love anywhere we want."

"Like to Mommy?" Heidi asks, her eyes wide with hope.

"Sure." Hillary smiles.

Heidi looks down at the shell in her hand, "Or maybe Daddy?"

Hillary reaches over, brushes seaweed off of Heidi's cheek and fights back tears. "Yes, even daddy."

The two go on gathering the other four stones. And they line them up—the white porous stone, a jet-black piece of petrified wood, a brownish red volcanic stone, a rounded smooth rock the size of a half dollar and a flat gray almost square rock.

Heidi digs her toes in the white sand while Hillary picks up a pearly, pink shell half, goes to the water's edge and fills it up. When she returns, she explains, "Sea water for anointing."

"What does that mean?" Heidi scoots in close.

Hillary uses her index finger to draw a five-pointed star in the sand. "Anointing is when we use oil or sea water as a way to connect us more deeply with ourselves and the ritual." She places the stones on each corner of the star and says, "I believe in the power of Water. The dolphin lives in water and breathes air and I am safe to create...."

"...and play." Heidi adds.

Smiling, Hillary nods and says, "Yes! Now put your hands on the sand like this and say, "The earth is my playground."

She takes the shell half, dips her middle finger in the seawater, anoints Heidi's forehead and the top of her feet with a small amount of seawater, "You are safe here and welcome in the game of life. Now you do the same for me." Heidi carefully takes the half shell and Hillary's forehead and feet.

Molly sits up, a look of worry clouding her face.

Oblivious to her sister's concern, Hillary lies back in the sand and makes a Sand Angel. Heidi is delighted and follows her aunt giggling with delight.

"Look at the sky and take four deep breaths." Hillary says.

Between fits of laughter and giggles, they both manage to inhale and exhale four times.

The two get up, wave their hands in the air and, upon Hillary's cue, run clock-wise three times around the circle shouting, "Wheeeeee!"

Hillary runs straight into the waves and falls face forward with a large splash.

Heidi runs in a large circle around her mother shouting and scattering sand, "Wheeeeee! I love the dolphins."

The waves roll over Hillary, dumping her face first on the ocean floor, and she is temporarily blinded. She wipes the stinging salt water and grains of sand from her eyes with her palms. When her vision clears, her first sight is Molly's face and stern expression.

Hillary exits the ocean in large steps, careful to avoid the glare in her wake that she senses.

On the ride back Heidi is chatty, reading every sign between the beach parking lot and their home.

"No loitering...Shelby's Donuts...Bruddah's...Oh, I like that place...Chase...why do they name a bank after a game?"

The sisters sit quietly. Their silence is punctuated by their occasional responses to Heidi's questions.

When they arrive home, Hillary quickly retreats to her private bathroom.

She pulls a large plastic bin from her bag, locks the door, unsnaps the lid to the bin to reveal an eclectic collection of essential oils and resins and settles on the edge of the tub.

She lovingly adjusts each vial of oil. Frankincense, Palmarosa, Chamomile, Dragon's Blood...each essence represents a doorway of healing. Her first experience with the healing properties of these oils came with the use of Dragon's Blood during her freshman year in high school.

Darla Melbert a "Threats" newbie had taken it upon herself to make an example of Hillary by calling her out as an oddball. Since they shared the same first period class, Darla's first order of business was to sit directly behind Hillary and quiz her loudly about her knowledge of the occult.

"Hey, Hillary." Darla whispered loudly. "I'll bet you know some pretty cool ways to bump people off."

Hillary did her best to remain cool. "Sorry, can't help you with that one, Darla."

"I don't really need your help," she would sneer and the entire class would prepare for the verbal assault that was coming. "What makes you so special?"

Hillary would put her nose in her book, but Darla would continue, "You're a know it all." Invariably, the teacher would be forced to intervene and send one or both of them to the office.

Hillary endured this abuse until Thanksgiving break. During a bustling holiday shopping trip with her mother, she wandered into a bookstore and headed straight for her favorite section Religion and Inspiration. Hillary loved to sit among these books and imagine the generations of people who fought, lived, loved and died to be heard. She identified with those who risk intolerance to say what might be considered unorthodox during their lifetime and felt protection within the literary confines of the bookstore. On this particular day, however, she walked up one side, then down the other running her hands over the book spines. Surely there was no solution to her protection issues at school within this aisle. She pulled several books and tucked herself into a space between shelves between Shinto and Taoism, but nothing resonated. She returned the books to the appropriate location and, disappointed, walked toward her mother. She listlessly perused the pocket sized gift books in the check out line as her mother chatted away about dinner plans. Then, she saw it. In a rack of moleskin diaries and joke books was the book that forever changed her life—simply titled, "Protection."

Over the break, that book went everywhere with Hillary. It contained the basics of what remains a pivotal element in her young life. Through rituals, oils and positive intention, protection was within her means. Most importantly, she discovered Dragon Oil is commonly used to uncross or remove hexes. It is a definitive protection oil that is distilled from the South American tree, Sangre de Drago and creates ultimate protection to increase power to the user.

On the first day back at school from Thanksgiving vacation, Hillary was armed with the small vial of Dragon's Blood oil. She had every intention of using it to anoint Darla's desk before class. All was still as Hillary stepped into the empty classroom, dabbed oil onto her finger, said a protective prayer for herself and the area surrounding it—just for good measure—then slipped out, fully intending to blend into the class as if she'd never been there. But, after rounding the corner at the end of the hallway, she stopped short.

"Did you hear about Darla Melbert?"

"No. What happened?"

Two senior girls, whom Hillary did not know, were at a locker, their heads close.

Hillary backed up behind the corner, out of sight but within earshot.

"Tried to kill herself during the break. I guess her dad was molesting her and her mom didn't believe it."

"How do you know?"

"My sister volunteers at the Mayfield County Hospital and saw the whole thing."

"Oh my God! Is she okay?"

"Well, she's still alive. They kept her in the Psych Ward for a few days then let her go."

"Wow, tough break. Anyway, what are you wearing to Shelby's party Friday?"

Stunned by the news, Hillary walked through the now crowded halls back to her first period class. Hillary slid in to her own desk behind Darla and found it hard to concentrate during the remainder of class.

The bell rang. Hillary followed Darla to her locker and touched her arm.

Darla turned, her eyes stony and said sharply, "What?"

Hillary handed Darla the Dragon oil and said simply, "For protection."

That was a turning point in Hillary's life. From that moment on, she vowed to right any wrongs to which she bore witness.

Hillary turns the shower on, adjusts the temperature then slips into the shower to wash off the day's sand and sunblock. Aside from sleep energy, the performing of mundane tasks—like showering—are the best times to approach and communicate with humans. So, I seize the moment and pop into the shower.

"Hello, Hillary." I say.

"Aaaaaahhhhh!" Hillary jumps and backs up against the wall. "Wwwhat? What are you doing here?"

"You have 72 hours to learn all there is to know to rescue Hawaii and all of humanity from certain doom."

"Oh, wow" Hillary sits awkwardly on the tile seat behind her, scattering plastic bottles of shampoo and conditioner.

The water hits her cheek and spray goes everywhere, but she does not seem to notice.

"Please know I don't mean to scare or harm you, only to inform you of a celestial opportunity."

"A celest...Look, Moa, I've come a long way in even acknowledging your presence. I'm not a psychic and I can't read energy. So can you please go find someone else to freak out while asking them to save the world?"

I know she is confused and scared. I will move as carefully as I can, given the extreme urgency, but she doesn't know what I know: Hillary is the only one who can open the portal and save Hawaii.

"Okay," I say patiently, "You have the power within you. I can prove it. Have you ever been sitting at a traffic light, sensed that someone is looking at you, turned to face them and they are?"

"Yes." The revelation begins.

"That power is within you! How could you possibly feel something from another person who is in a completely different car unless you..."

A loud knock interrupts our visit.

"Hillary?" It's Molly and she doesn't sound pleased.

"Yes."

"Can I come in?"

"Sure." Hillary throws her hands up in desperation. Her privacy has been encroached by an entity. What's the difference if her sister comes in? "Why not? Come join the party." Hillary stands, letting the warm water flow over her, hoping it can give her some courage and clarity.

Molly comes in and sits down on the commode opposite the shower. The two women lock eyes through the fogged-over glass shower door. I blend into the shower mist. Molly is furious as she confronts her pruney sister. "Who's Moa?"

As Hillary shifts her weight from one foot to the next, a dribble of soap curls down the drain around her right foot. With a visible gulp she begins, "I had a dream and this little girl appeared to deliver a message that Steve is okay."

"How does Heidi know about this?"

"Um...let's see, I might have sent Moa to Heidi...

"You what!" Molly stands up and puts her face inches from the shower door.

Hillary fearfully backs up. "I...I was sleepy and didn't believe her...but it all just...."

"Stop it! Do not tell my sweet little girl ridiculous non-sense. No spells, no witchcraft, no more make-believe rituals. I will not allow this in my house." Molly stomps off slamming the bathroom door.

I ride the steamy wave of mist back to my spot in front of Hillary who is welling with tears.

"All is well." I send a whirl of calming blue energy to her head. I am able to intervene with humans if I am the cause of worry or upset or, heaven forbid, someone is in harm's way.

Once she has calmed down, she says, "Do you have some kind of fascination with my morning ablutions?" The distress lifts from the top of her head in a wisp of gray smoke, which curls past the ceiling and dissipates.

"No," I smile, "I'm just catching you at the perfect vibration."

"So when I'm showering, I'm at the perfect vibration to speak with you?"

"Yes. You are relaxed enough to feel, see and understand me."

"How do I explain this to my sister?"

"Here is what you say to your sister: My ancient world and your world—earth—are very similar to watching television with a DVR. Both worlds co-exist and going between them is as easy as switching the tuner."

"Genius! Now, if I agree to work with you, may I please finish my shower?"

I leave her to rinse and repeat in peace.

Dinner is a feast of local fare. They found a variety of lau lau—chicken, beef, pork or, Hillary's favorite—salted butterfish wrapped in Taro or Ti leaves. Molly steamed white rice—one of the island staples, along with macaroni salad. Before Steve passed on, he showed Hillary a way to make the meal even more delicious by drizzling a little shoyu onto the rice and macaroni salad before eating. Just as it is with her essential oils, when mayonnaise and soy sauce mix, two very different flavors create a fabulous new one!

As Hillary shakes the shoyu over her food, she thinks of Steve and his warm humor and happy grin. His gift of gab has definitely rubbed off on his daughter.

Heidi is munching on some carrots and peppering her mother with a barrage of questions/statements.

"How come I have to eat carrots? Auntie doesn't have to?"

"Because Aunt Hillary is grown."

"She's not a grown up."

"I didn't say…"

"Moa is wise and she's not a grown up." Heidi shoots a piercing defiant stare at Molly.

Molly, in turn, glares at Hillary.

With only two and a half days to go, I decide, enough's enough and I blow a gust of air against the curtains of the living room. The filmy drape creates a perfect backdrop for me—my shape distinctly outlined, my face clearly shows up and they all see me. All three mouths gape as the thin veil of our two worlds bridge.

CHAPTER VI

The Container

Ritual: Moa's Healing Light
Oil: Base of Apricot Oil – Fennel, Lavender, Neroli
Incense: Lavender
Incantation: "I create grace."

Light the Lavender and allow it to burn. Anoint your third eye, throat and base of spine. Lie in a dimly lit room where you will not be disturbed. Inhale deeply and visualize breathing in a healing light. Exhale slowly through your mouth and see any illness, negativity, discomfort, disease leaving your body going back to source. Continue breathing and visualizing healing light until you can no longer see any more illness, discomfort or disease to exhale. Imagine the healing light is surrounding your entire body and extending one foot around. Relax in the healing light for as long as you wish.

You are healed. Inhale light, exhale to release.
Know healing is within your power.

✛

"Moa! Hey...Mom, look! It's Moa." Heidi is the first to speak.

Molly continues to stare, still trying to deny what she is seeing. I blow another gust so the material surrounds and outlines me and I intone, "Molly, your future and that of your daughter, depends on Hillary's participation. Please support her in her quest to save Hawaii. Time is of the essence. If you agree, meet me in Thomas Square Park and I'll show you what to do." I complete my gusty call and retire to the lofty banyan treetops while the women intensely discuss their next move.

"Let's go," Hillary begins to rummage through the kitchen drawers.

"What are you doing?" Molly's voice is tinged with anger.

"I'm going to meet Moa at the park." Hillary continues to open and close doors.

Heidi joins her in the search and unearths her dad's old flashlight from a broom closet. "Found one!"

"Um, no you're not." Molly rises and clenches her fists. "I'm not exactly sure what just happened, but I am positive, I'm not going to follow whatever that was into a dark and dangerous park."

Hillary also finds the flashlight under the sink and heads toward the front door. However, Molly is not going down this easy and blocks the way.

"C'mon, Mom," Heidi stamps her foot. "Moa needs our help!"

Hillary knows exactly how to handle this type of situation. "Mol, she's just a child who desperately needs our help." The second Molly lets her guard down, Hillary and Heidi are out the door. Then, Hillary calls behind her as she descends the stairs, "Plus you can be there to protect us."

Ever dedicated to making sure her sister and daughter are safe, Molly reaches for a weapon and sprints toward Thomas Square Park.

As I watch Hillary, Molly, and Heidi enter the circle of trees, I am reminded of how much I miss being human. Many of the ancients have either never been on earth or haven't been in human form for thousands of years. When this urge overtakes me, I move into someone's body. Not for very long, of course—and always after asking permission—but long enough to taste an ice cream cone, feel the pull of the ocean against skin or sense the tingle of an impending rain shower. Don't get me wrong. I truly enjoy being a non-being—moving through portals, telepathy and traveling beyond material confines allows for some multi-dimensional fun as does escorting souls from the confines of their earthly bodies into the joyous, welcoming Light. But, there are moments when I wish I could live in my body again. For all the pain that encompasses a human's life, it is all worth a joyful laugh with a friend. It is because of my practice of inhabiting human's, albeit, briefly, that I am able to achieve my next feat.

Heidi, dressed for the occasion, wears a beautiful red and yellow Japanese kimono and carries a flashlight that is slightly smaller than her entire left arm. Molly has a matching flashlight and the first thing she could grab in case of trouble—a sparkly purple six-inch platform shoe from Heidi's dress-up chest by the front door. I'll give her this, the spiked heel certainly looks like a weapon. Hillary turns on a lantern and in a far corner of the park, a homeless man, nested in a pile of blankets snores vociferously.

"What are we supposed to do?" Heidi, ever curious, asks a little too loudly.

"Shhhh…" Cautions Hillary.

"Hello." While the group has been discussing, I have "moved in" to the man's body. He, thankfully, agreed to allow me to speak briefly to my friends while he snoozed away. Although unorthodox, this practice allows me to be seen by those who cannot normally communicate with an entity like me. Humans are blessed with a variety of senses including extrasensory perception. And although every human possesses the ability to "see"—beyond their normal vision—what is around them, many refuse to acknowledge that ability or those things just beyond their normal five senses can experience.

"Sir. Please leave us alone." Molly tightens her grip on her unlikely weapon—now behind her back—and keeps her voice even.

"No need to fear. It is I, Moa."

"Hey, it is Moa." Heidi bends down and tries to look up the man's nose, then peeks into his ears, trying to find any trace of me. "What are you doing in there?"

"This is the only way I can communicate with all of you at once." I feel a little unsteady in my borrowed body, so I sit on a stone wall next to the group.

"What do we do first? It's late and I want to get Heidi into bed soon." Molly says, a weary note of resignation in her voice.

"The first thing to remember is that energy comes from within you. Your power begins by asking, believing and thanking. The asking comes in the form of a simple, clear and well-worded question."

64

"Not hard to do at this point." Hillary pulls out a pen and pad from her back pack and begins writing.

"Then comes the believing...true belief means holding and locking in the highest vibration for your outcome. Molly and Heidi, I've asked for Hillary's help in opening the portal to my home. It has been closed and—as powerful as I am—I cannot reopen it without your help. Hillary can explain how this all came to pass. In the meantime, I need for you all to agree to help me and to follow my instructions to the letter."

"Lock in a vibration?" Hillary puts down the pen and shoves back the pad. "I have no idea what you mean."

Molly crosses her arms across her chest, "Whoever or whatever you are, there is no way I'll ever understand your world or how to save it. Let's go." She takes Heidi by the hand and walks away from us.

"Okay, right there." I raise my voice, but Molly continues to walk out of the park. "What you just said, Molly. Words are extremely powerful. Imagine that positive emotions are higher and negative emotions are lower. When you said 'there is no way I'll ever understand' that causes a lower vibration and you've locked it in with the words. You are most assuredly going to have a negative outcome—and your words will come true! You will never understand. But, if you do want to understand, then all you need to do is change those words and lock in the new higher, more positive vibration."

This hits a nerve with Molly, who stops and turns back. "Are you telling me that all I have to do is believe and nothing bad will ever happen?" Her voice drips with sarcasm and Heidi tries to calm her mother by moving close and grabbing her hand.

"No. Being human includes many challenges and bad things do happen. Molly, I know your husband is no longer here on this earth, but you must believe that he exists, just not here on earth. If you hold the thought of hope, then you increase your ability to process joy.

However, you can make things worse by continuing to lock in a negative vibration. It's okay to be sad and to feel sad, but it is also okay to feel love and joy. These are all emotions you humans hold within your bodies. If you lock in grief and sadness for a long time, you can almost guarantee difficulty!"

"You have no idea." Molly mutters.

I ignore her and turn to Hillary. "It may sound too simple, but by merely breathing deeply and relaxing and aligning with your higher self by clearing your body, mind and spirit, Hillary, you will be able to open the locked portal."

Then I turn to Molly, "Heidi is in danger. If you truly want to protect her, you'll listen to what I have to say. Now sit!"

Molly, reeling from my words, flops down on the wall next to me. "Now that I have your attention, know this. You are about to embark on a journey beyond your current realm of knowledge. I am here, in part, to protect you and ensure your safe voyage. Now, close your eyes, both eyes, Molly, and imagine," I say, "that you have a red spinning ball at the bottom of your spine. See a light clearing it and allow it to spin freely. Now, take in a long breath through your nose and let it out slowly in a breathy, "Ahhhh." I direct them to do this three times.

"That is all for tonight." I say. Then I place my "temporary container" back in the nest of musty blankets and drift skyward.

Molly, Hillary and Heidi exchange puzzled looks and shrugs. "What was that all about?" Molly hisses. However, they are too exhausted for any more mysteries and head home for the night and some much-needed uninterrupted sleep.

"Pssst. Aunt Hillary." A little hand touches her forehead, and then a giggle follows. Hillary feels a tickle on her nose and opens her eyes to find Heidi holding a feather over her face. Heidi bounces on the mattress sending covers and sheets tumbling onto the hardwood floor. "Look what I found!"

It is morning—only 48 hours to go in our earth saving quest—and last night at the park seems years ago. Hillary groggily sits up to get a better look at this new found object. "Where did you find it?" Hillary asks.

"On the kitchen counter." Heidi skips off to her room to get ready for today's adventure.

The feather is brown with black flecks and about a foot long. Hillary stumbles into the bathroom and tries to imagine what kind of bird would produce such a grand feather.

Just as she sits down on the commode, I pop in.

Hillary jumps then relaxes, "Oh, hi Moa. What's going on?"

"I wanted to find out how you are feeling?"

"Okay. I guess." Hillary's head is in her hands.

"I want to suggest sending you on a telepathic healing journey to prepare you for what lies ahead."

"Okay, I..." before she finishes her sentence, Hillary is walking down a long country road.

It is a crisp fall day. She breathes in the earthy smell of fall. The leaves are changing, the grass is drying and up ahead she sees a cabin. She decides to go inside. As she steps into the cabin, she notices a flight of stairs leading into the basement. A warm glow beckons her from the depths of the staircase and she slowly descends the stairs. As her feet touch the dirt-covered basement floor, she sees a ruby red chair sitting next to a small round table. On the table is a small votive candle. That candle is providing all the light and warmth for this room. She moves to the chair and sits down. The ruby chair is comfortable and smooth. As she sits, she feels the chair pulling any fear, anger and insecurities from the base of her spine.

I speak clearly, "The release comes in any form you choose, Hillary: A clear tube, a single thread or a light beam. Allow this energy to move from you through your conduit deep into the earth. Once it hits the earth, it immediately dissipates. Take your time and express any feelings that rise to move through and out of you."

When Hillary is finished, a shaft of light appears overhead. It moves over the chair and she feels a divine light filling her feet, legs and lower region with healing warm light.

"Let the light heal and soothe you." I say kindly. "Take in the renewing loving energy. When you are done, thank the Light and rise from the chair."

The stairs are now glowing with Life-force and as she takes the first step to ascend, Hillary feels a tingle through her entire body. Just as she reaches for the doorknob to exit the cabin into the crisp autumn dusk, she hears my voice once more, "Turn and meet Ula Ula. She is an Anuenue and welcomes you to your first level of clearing." A beautiful Inuit woman with silvery hair and a red robe puts her hand on Hillary's heart and nods. Hillary nods back and proceeds out the door feeling stronger and more centered than ever before.

Hillary feels herself back in the bathroom. She is still seated on the commode, her legs numb and tingling from lack of blood flow.

"Well, Moa, you sure know how to keep things interesting," Hillary says, rubbing her legs to wake them up. Just then she hears Molly crying.

She exits the bathroom, wanders out into the hall and into Molly's bedroom where her sister is sitting on her bed, her face in her hands. "What's the matter? Has something happened?"

"I saw Steve." Molly heaves and hiccups two more times before continuing, "Moa took me on a journey and before I could protest, I was back at Big Bear in the ski lodge. Remember? We went there for our first anniversary."

Hillary realizes Molly had a "clearing" too!

Molly sniffs, then. "I feel so much better. Like I got another hug goodbye."

The two sisters hold each other until Heidi comes into the room with the feather. "Hey, I figured out what this is for. This morning I was getting dressed and then all of a sudden I remembered my map. Come on, I'll show you. Hurry up!"

Heidi skips up the stairs with Hillary and Molly in tow, then pulls a large laminated map of Honolulu from her overflowing toy chest. "We have to take the feather, do the Huna Prayer and let the feather go on top of Diamond Head."

Remembering my words about Heidi being in danger, Molly reluctantly says, "Well, I wanted to go for a hike, anyway."

The women stuff a backpack full of all hiking necessities: water, sunblock, snacks…Heidi carefully places the feather in her own school backpack and they head out.

The hike is a steep one, although Heidi navigates it effortlessly. Molly goes first and scouts the best route to the top. Heidi is second and Hillary follows behind the group to ensure Heidi does not fall.

CHAPTER VII

The Power of Air

Ritual: Truth
Oil: Base of Grape Seed Oil – Rosewood, Chamomile, Vetiver
Incense: Sweet Grass
Incantation: "I heal my heart."

Burn the sweet grass as you anoint your heart with the oil. Bring your palms together in prayer position at your heart and say the incantation. Close your eyes and imagine sheer curtains in front of you. Know that your truth is behind the curtains and if you part them, it will be forever, irrevocably revealed. Your personal freedom is beyond those curtains. Reach out and pull them away to see what lies beyond.
Truth is a precious gift. Know that you are free to see your truth.

The top of Diamond Head is flat and narrow, and hikers can walk unimpeded right out to the terrifying edge. I am waiting at the peak when the group arrives.

"Must be nice." Hillary says.

"What do you mean?" Molly cannot see or hear me.

I'm sitting on a rock at the edge of the lookout. There are no rails or curbs, just a steep drop straight down the mountain.

"Moa, how did you get here so fast?" Heidi takes a step closer to me and Molly intervenes to keep her from walking any closer.

"Hey!" Molly cries out.

"This time I soared with a seagull." I say. Heidi watches as I jump off the rock's edge, throw my arms out wide and circle around their heads before coming to rest on the rock again.

"Hey Mom, Moa didn't have to hike at all. She flew!" With that Heidi jumps up as if she is ready for take off, but I instantly send a charged light field in front of her. This type of protective field is invisible to but impenetrable by humans.

"Don't ever try this, Heidi. I am not human but you most certainly are!" I say sternly. "That means you are breakable!"

Heidi peers over the edge at the sharp rocks below, her face showing surprise as she contemplates a fall. "Wow," she says. "I promise I won't!" Heidi turns to her mother, busies herself with helping unpack the snacks.

There is no vegetation at the top, no trees or plants of any kind. Once the three have made it to the top of Diamond Head, Hillary finds a protected area between two boulders and sets up a small picnic. A cotton blanket makes a perfect seating area and she arranges two bananas and two apples—one red and one green, cheese and crackers as well as water at far corner of the blanket.

Molly grabs a red apple, wipes it on her shirt and walks to the edge of the precipice where her daughter stood only moments before and calmly surveys the bird's eye view of the gorgeous arc of beach extending toward Pearl Harbor. Two sailboats cut through the glistening sea, sails fully open and an enormous ocean liner clings to the horizon. "It's been a long time since we've done this hike, right Heidi?"

"Waikiki beach looks so little from way up here. I remember Daddy used to put me on his shoulders and I would be taller than the mountain..." Heidi trails off, then rises and moves close to her mother. "Sure is steep." The wind picks up, pulling at their clothes.

"What should we do with the feather?" Heidi asks. A powerful gust pushes at them, nearly causing the child to lose her balance.

"Moa, is that you?" Heidi yells and takes a backward step away from the cliff.

"No." I say. I try to keep my voice even. Although I don't want to scare her, I have a strong sense this force is definitely sinister, but since I am cloaked and don't want to be discovered, I cannot investigate further and identify the source. When I am cloaked, I essentially go into "stillpoint" a non-vibrational state. When this happens, I am unable to do anything but stay put.

Another step produces a frightening cold blast in the form of a wind gust, sending them running for cover toward their protected snack area.

"Go home!" The wind screeches.

"What was that?" Hillary yells as the wind increases.

The Hawaiian Islands contain powerful channels for energy—both negative and positive. These naturally occurring channels come in the form of vortexes, which are essentially energetic conduits through which energy is transferred. Portals and vortexes are similar, however, portals are used for travel between the worlds and vortexes are used as energy emitters. The Bermuda Triangle, where ships and planes have mysteriously disappeared, is an especially powerful vortex. Hawaii has its own version of the Bermuda Triangle, northeast of The Big Island. A volcano called Hamakulia contains a vortex with mysterious powers.

Hawaiian's believed that Pele, goddess of the volcano, harnessed the power within Hawaiian volcanoes as a channel for her own anger. She is known for her fiery tirades and massive destructive outbursts in the form of earthquakes and eruptions. The Hekili are Anuenue who turned to Pele and use anger to fuel their power. I believe Pele is behind the huge blasts of anger directed toward Heidi, Hillary and Molly, and I use my own version of Mana—power of the breath, life force or chi— which is called Peko—to redirect the wind away from Heidi, Molly and Hillary.

Fearing for her life, Hillary crouches down on the closest flat boulder she can find, puts her hands over her head, closes her eyes and calls to Moa. Her voice is barely audible through the howling gale, "Help us, Moa! Where are you?"

Molly and Heidi cling to one another, crying in the shelter of a large boulder. They are both too frightened to speak.

I decide to get them out of there fast. With a flash, they are walking in the sand at the edge of the ocean. It is a comfortable evening, the stars are out and they walk calmly on the sand. The only way I can combat a negative energy blast, such as the one Heidi, Hillary and Molly experienced, is to identify the source. Then I am able to shift or move the situation to a more desirable location. Removing the group from the source of negativity on Diamond Head's peak was the best I could do.

"What happened?" Heidi whispers. She still clutches the feather in one hand.

"I think Moa helped us by sending us here." Hillary says.

"At least we're all together." Molly sits down on the sand. "But I'm not going anywhere until I know where I am..."

Suddenly, a column of gold light appears about ten feet ahead. The three carefully approach this amazing phenomenon. And as they near this unusual sight, they see a shimmering golden staircase, which leads down into the sand.

"Hey, check it out." The stairs are unlit, but Hillary notices a flashlight next to the first step.

"Come on, Mom." Heidi grabs the flashlight and heads down the gilded stairs.

The rail is encrusted with precious jewels and, although apprehensive, the group has a sense that they are protected.

My voice reverberates through the mouth of the staircase. "If you continue, you will gain personal knowledge beyond comprehension and spiritual gems beyond monetary meas...."

Before I can I finish, a booming authoritative voice cuts me off. "You will never know the truth."

The women and Heidi are frozen and unable to speak. I am sure they will, once again, be rendered speechless when they find out that this fearsome soul is a relative, their own flesh and blood.

"Look, Lord Paulet. You have experienced many setbacks during your time on earth. We understand that you wished to reign over Hawaii, but that time has passed and we wish for you to have the freedom to come and go as you desire." I speak for them.

Then, I create a large blue bubble around each of them and say, "The fiery spirit which wishes you harm is your great-great-great grandfather. His name is Lord George Paulet."

Hillary interrupts, "You mean we are related to the man who took over the Hawaiian Islands and overthrew King Kahmehameha III?"

"Yes, you were drawn to Thomas Square Park for a reason. Listen with tempered judgment. He is an angry entity and continues to cultivate the lower emotions with his fire. Use the flashlight and walk in protection. The anger is only talk. It can no longer hurt you. I will not go any farther into these halls with you. You must go alone. This is your journey of self discovery. I'll be waiting for you upon your return."

Hillary takes the flashlight and they walk closely to each other descending the stairs carefully. Molly takes thoughtful steps while holding the rail tightly, while Hillary and Heidi move much more quickly toward the end. As they step off at the bottom, the flashlight catches a dark image.

"Stand behind me!" Hillary directs Molly and Heidi, then demands in a strong voice, "Show yourself!"

"Nice one, Hil." Molly says encouragingly, and Hillary can hear the smile in her voice.

"Thanks," she says then she smiles to herself. It feels good to have her older sister acknowledge her bravery.

Hillary continues her steady gaze at the apparition and speaks in a clear, even tone, "Show yourself."

Lord George Paulet appears in full dress uniform. He wears a navy waistcoat with large gold double-breasted buttons connected with braided gold ribbons and crisply ironed long blue trousers. He stands with a tall tufted hat under his arm and puffs his chest out before he unfurls his wrath upon and around the group. Instead of words, he shoots fiery blasts at them. Even though I've told them they'll be protected, the show of anger increases each person's level of fear.

Lord Paulet had been using Pele just as the Hekili did—for his own negative use. No matter, where trouble is, Pele is not far behind.

Absolutely flummoxed, Molly yells, "Hillary, what should we do?" She pulls her daughter close to her side.

"The feather!" Heidi shouts, still clutching it in her small sweaty fist..

"Lord Paulet's anger was the source of the gusts at Diamond Head's peak. Your Granddad has focused his anger through Pele as a Hekili. You have the power to do for yourself," I say. "Place the feather on the ground and create a protective chamber as I did for you. Imagine it and it is so. Quickly!"

Much to everyone's surprise, Paulet is immediately encased in a clear blue box. He struggles to escape by banging on the blue walls to no avail. And disappointed, he slumps down in the bottom of the case.

They walk farther down the hallway, feeling safe with the knowledge that Granddad can no longer frighten them.

Suddenly, an ornate wooden door with inlaid fleur de lis and carved angels appears right in front of them, and Hillary touches the knob, then says knowingly, "I don't know how I know this, but Lord Paulet has a message for us."

Heidi lovingly touches Hillary's shoulder. "It's Moa, she sent you a mental message. She's done that with me sometimes. It sounds like a whisper right next to my ear, but when I look, no one is there."

Molly's expression suddenly changes, "Wait! I don't think we should go in there. How do we know that this isn't a trick? What if we get in that room and he harms us?"

"If we don't go in, what do we do? Granddad will continue to harass us." Hillary says this and both she and Heidi stare intently at Molly waiting for an answer.

"Fine. But if something happens..." Molly grumbles her unfinished threat and the three open the door and enter a smartly decorated room. Hillary takes a look around and decides it most closely resembles their grandparents' house in Florida—loads of potted plants, wicker furniture and tile floors. The air is warm and moist, but the tile floors radiate cool. The result is a comfortable, summerhouse feel. As she takes in the atmosphere, Hillary discovers a box in the far corner of the room. The box pulses with vibrant light through the opaque resin and Hillary runs her fingers over the smooth top and sides. She can see tiny insects and bugs that were once trapped in the resin thousands of years ago encased in the wondrous material.

"Is that amber?" Heidi asks.

Hillary nods. "I think so."

"Let's open it." Molly wants to know what's inside.

"I think our fear has a message for us." Heidi whispers. "I learned about amber in school. It can trap and preserve bugs for thousands and thousands..."

"Heidi, love, let's focus on what's inside the box," says Molly. Shocked by her own intuitive revelation, she adds, "The source of fear is embedded in our DNA—from the grandfather who desperately wants us to leave."

Hillary adds, "Our genes were written in fear. Open the box."

"Another Moa message?" Molly asks.

Hillary nods solemnly and then proceeds with caution. As she slowly opens the box, a warm gush of air escapes along with a hiss. The moldy scent of decaying paper encircles them.

"Wow, it's almost like we're uncovering some ancient family secret." Hillary says.

"I know..." Molly replies.

Interrupting their conversation is a loud rush more noise than air, and suddenly, a see-through image of the fearful grandfather appears between them.

"Go home!" he booms.

This time, however, his words are far less ominous because, although Lord Paulet is dressed in full war regalia. His epaulets shimmer with an ethereal glow and he sports Heidi's dress-up six-inch sparkly platform shoes.

I couldn't help inserting my own fashion choice. After all, serves him right for frightening these three wonderful women.

However, he is yet unaware of his attire and continues his thunderous tirade. "You must leave and never return."

"Hey, those are mine!" Heidi squeals, pointing to her shoes.

The group stifles giggles and, it is then that Granddad discovers his disco duds. A look of shock, then embarrassment washes over Granddad's craggy face. His image fades until only his face is visible and with renewed anger he continues, "Beware..." in his best menacing voice, but the sinister effect has been lost and Hillary, Molly and Heidi dissolve into laughter.

Overcome with embarrassment, Granddad disappears entirely, and without another word, a small puff of smoke curls in his place.

Hillary closes the box's lid and the two make their way out of the room into the dimly lit hallway, as they round a corner, they see Granddad reappeared, in a more solid form still wearing war regalia up top and Heidi's purple platforms below, sitting with his back against the wall, shoulders hunched and heaving in sobs.

Molly is the first to reach him, and places a hand on his shoulder. Without looking up, he speaks, "Please understand, I wish no more than to protect my family. All humans on the Hawaiian Islands will perish if there is unrestricted access to the Ancient portal."

"Why?" Hillary kneels to his level, as do Heidi and Molly.

"After Admiral Thomas' reinstated King Kahmehameha's reign, I entered the Ancient Portal and have not been able to return to earth since. If I am not on earth to protect the gallant citizens of Hawaii, they will become impoverished and die. When I first arrived on the Island, King Kahmehameha had driven Hawaii's economy into the ground. After I took over, the people rejoiced at the changes I made. I supported trade and commerce in a way that that savage King never could. And I would have continued if it wasn't for that meddler, Admiral Thomas and your friend, Moa."

"What does Moa have to do with your captivity?" Hillary asks.

"She will not let me out!" Lord Paulet wails.

"That can't be true." Molly kneels now, too. "Moa is a kind soul who wants universal access so that humans can use free will to choose when it is their time."

"Just ask her." Granddad sighs. "I'm trapped. When you find out the truth, you'll want what I want, what is best for our family."

Unable to come up with a way to show reverence to someone she cannot touch, Hillary opts for a low curtsey. Molly and Heidi follow her lead.

"Dear Lord Paulet, thank you for passing the message to us. We receive it with respect and..." Hillary cannot think of the words to finish.

But Molly helps her along, "...and love. Yes, thank you Granddad."

Heidi comes out of her curtsy and smiles widely. And, much to his relief, I restore Lord Paulet's dress uniform to its original state—sans disco sparkle.

The group continues down the dark, winding hallway with walls of large limestone block toward a light, chattering with happy relief. They reach another stairway leading up and ascend quickly, skipping and hopping up the stairs to the soft sand and the roar of crashing waves.

"Granddad is a misguided soul. Moa told me that he is trapped between the worlds and mistakenly follows his quest to conquer this portal the way he tried to overtake Hawaii." Hillary finds a soft divot in the sand and settles in, Molly and Heidi do the same—grateful for the break.

They take a moment to quietly watch the water ebb and flow, the tide pulling at the beach and stirring the sand.

"The waves sound different." Heidi breaks the silence staring into the horizon.

"How so?" Molly doesn't take her eyes off of the water, either.

"The crashing sound of waves used to remind me of thunder. Now it reminds me of Daddy. I am not worried about where he is anymore. He's okay, and so are we."

Molly scoots over and holds her daughter in a long embrace.

I follow them back home sending my light energy to a spot onto a wicker rocking chair on Molly's lanai, then I slowly fill in with my own opaque matter. This is my favorite way to travel—smooth and easy.

Hillary leads the way up the stairs of the house, the beautiful cool evening following them inside. The beds beckon from the bedrooms and after a quick brushing of teeth and washing of faces, they are all drifting off in a restorative, calm rest. I stay close, ensuring that they remain undisturbed.

CHAPTER VIII

Trust

Ritual: Release of Embedded Fear

Oil: Base of Jojoba Oil – Coriander, Fennel, Ginger, Valerian

Incense: Dried Lavender

Incantation: "I have all I need to proceed."

Sit in the light of the Full Moon. Anoint your heart and the base of your spine with the oil. Also, anoint the barbeque or urn and the area around which you will be doing this ritual. Write your worst fears on slips of paper. Burn these slips in either a barbeque or small fire-safe urn. As you burn each slip, repeat the incantation. Your fears will be released, never to return.

Proceed with confidence and joy. Know that when fears arise, you may repeat this ritual and release them at will.

After a good night's sleep, and a sustaining breakfast of scrambled eggs and cheese, country ham and warm corn muffins the group is ready to open the portal to the Ancient world.

"I don't get it." Heidi takes Hillary's hand as they cross the street, "Why is Granddad so angry?"

"He is desperate to return to his old life—the one in which he was a powerful leader." Hillary says as they walk onto the stone path that leads to the patio on Thomas Square.

"But Sir Thomas gave King Kamehameha back his job as ruler of Hawaii." Heidi stays close to her mom and Hillary.

"Desperation can do funny things to people. It can even make people rewrite history and live in an altered place. That's what happened to Granddad. He still mistakenly thinks he can come back and rule Hawaii—and that we can somehow help him. Well, we can help him go into a less desperate place so he finally see where and who he is."

"How do we do that?" Heidi follows Hillary to a spot on the patio where the morning sun streams through the trees.

"We can do the Huna Prayer and get as clear as possible within ourselves about where and who we are." Hillary says. "Let's sit here in the sun."

The circle of banyan trees provides a protected dome over the center of the patio where they will perform the Huna Prayer. The morning dew provides a cool feeling even though they sit in direct sunlight. Hillary breathes deeply and slowly in for five beats, holds for three beats, then breathes out for seven. Molly and Heidi watch Hillary and follow her lead. Soon the group is breathing peacefully and they have raised their vibration.

I join the group and can see this beautiful increased vibration as ribbons of golden energy flowing around each person's head, torso and feet. Transformation is one of my favorite pieces to observe from the human experience. Lower vibrations—like fear and desperation show up as jagged shards of red and black. When a human calms, and her energy turns into golden ribbons, it is an incredible sight to behold.

Granddad, however, has other plans. In the middle of their praying, large drops of rain begin to fall and soon torrents of water pour through holes in the banyan's green canopy.

"You will not open the Ancient Portal. The family lineage is committed to protecting access to the portal," roars Granddad.

"If the family lineage is so committed, then where are they?" Molly whispers loudly under her breath.

Angered by Molly's display of disrespect, Granddad thunders, "You have two minutes to leave the premises or face the consequences."

"Or what?" Heidi says with no trace of fear.

"I will remind you that you are on earth now, not within the energetic confines of one of Moa's visioning trips. I am powerful here on earth." His voice shakes the earth beneath their feet and causes the stone wall to shudder and crack. "You will obey me or Admiral Thomas's spawn will pay!" With a sharp cackle he then sends a streak of lightening that explodes just above their heads."

"Okay," Hillary says, "That was certainly real, and way too close for comfort."

The banyans naturally grow toward the sky then send shoots from the tallest tree limbs back to earth embedding them deeply in the dark earth. When this happens, a new tree begins to grow. This circle of trees are created and recreated throughout the past 100 years and now have a circuitous network of vertical limbs, which, in turn have safe pockets. The three of them scramble into a shelter that had been formed by two intertwining banyan limbs.

Heidi stifles a giggle. "I keep picturing him with my purple platforms. Why is he still so angry, Moa?"

I hover protectively in the entrance of the alcove. "He still harbors anger toward Admiral Thomas," I say. "Because Lord Paulet wanted to continue to reign over the Hawaiian Islands instead of King Kahmehameha. Admiral Thomas made sure that would never happen by thwarting his efforts and restoring the true King back to power. What he doesn't understand is that the way he originally accessed the portal was through his own free will. No one forced him to go through. And he is able to exit any time by the same will. The key to his freedom however, is in releasing his misguided quest to "save his family" through keeping a vigilant watch over the Portal. All that has resulted in his vigilance is more suffering.

His powers are limited to moving weather around and crashing trees but I'll stick with you just to make sure you stay safe."

"But, Moa," Hillary whispers, "doesn't that mean that if everyone who passes on can move freely through the Ancient Portal that you'll be out of a job."

Granddad's voice booms in a thunderous anger shaking the trees and rattling the limbs that form their protective nook. "How dare you bring Admiral Thomas's spawn into my presence! You mock our lineage and thus me."

"Well, yes, but don't worry..." I begin, but before I can finish, Granddad sneaks a sinewy tree limb behind Heidi, which he wraps around Heidi's waist and ankles. Within seconds, Heidi disappears into a new portal, which dissolves instantly. I realize with a shock that I have no idea where this one goes. There are few times when I am at a loss about what to do. This is one. Could I have underestimated Granddad's power? It looks as if he is able to not only move himself but apparently humans through to other dimensions as well.

Hillary and Molly run to the earthy spot begin to dig and claw at the ground to no avail. Molly screams Heidi's name until she is hoarse. Hillary desperately screams at Granddad. Both cling to each other and cry.

In the darkness, Heidi blinks, too stunned to even cry.
Then she says cautiously, "Moa?"
"I'm here, Heidi."
Although I am not able to go into my own portal, as luck would have it I can access this new one. I follow her and create a suitably safe place within the confines of "inner space." We are somewhere deep within the earth, but the only way out is the way in, through the original opening. And Granddad has locked the entrance.
"I know. I can feel you." The brave youngster remains remarkably calm when any other child might be reduced to screaming and tears. She takes a deep breath and asks, "Can you please make it light?"
"Sure."
Instantly, we are in an empty room a crackling fire in the fireplace is the source of light. The warmth from the fire sends a flow of calmness through Heidi's body.

"Why don't you lie here?" I point to a soft mat that I materialize from my childhood memory. It is woven and tufted cotton.

Heidi settles down next to this soothing powerful fire, and is soon asleep.

After Heidi and I were taken away, I managed to send Hillary and Molly somewhere safe and did my best to duplicate Heidi's surroundings.

Their fire cracks and sparks. Hillary stares helplessly into the flames. Molly is next to her, in deep shock. Since I'm not exactly sure where Heidi and I are, I cannot bring Hillary and Molly to us. Where are they? It's hard to explain. Better to say they aren't with Heidi and I, but they can't be harmed by their Granddad either. They are in their parallel "inner space" between the worlds.

"Molly." Hillary follows an errant spark as it drifts up.

"Where are we?" Molly says stoically.

"I don't know, but I feel like Moa and Heidi are close by."

The two women look around for a door, each woman in her own unique way. A smooth slate gray rock face surrounds them. The only illumination is the fire in the center of the room. Hillary helps her sister explore the area looking for any means of escape. She is methodical in her search and begins at one end of their walled space from top to bottom.

Molly is exhausted and distraught and paces the length of the space wringing her hands. The more she looks, the more agitated Molly gets.

Finally, she pounds the rock wall and begins to sob. "I just want my baby back."

"I still don't understand why he would take Heidi." Hillary puts her arms around her sister and fights back tears as they both gaze into the fire.

"Wait. Granddad was infuriated that we brought Admiral Thomas's spawn. Neither one of us is related to Admiral Thomas..."

Molly finishes her sisters thought, "...and neither is Moa because she hasn't been on earth since before the Paulet Affair."

"Heidi!" Molly jumps up. "Oh, Hillary, that means that Steve was related to Admiral Thomas!"

Molly pulls on Hillary's arm. "C'mon, let's go! We have to get out of here, we have to find them, now that we know why he has Heidi! She is the closest genetic connection to Admiral Thomas! We must tell Granddad that the Paulet Affair happened a long time ago and he can let Heidi go."

"Mol, there is no way out I can find through these walls, but..." Hillary is determined to find a solution.

"She's just a little girl!" Molly's body is rigid. She clenches her fists in frustration.

Staring into the fire, Hillary gets an idea, "This fire represents release. I created a circle with my friends in school with some powerful results. I think we can do the same thing here. Whatever we put into this fire will forever be transformed and released from our bodies, minds and spirits. We must make a list of words." She grabs a pad that appears near her hand. "Write items that represent things you would like to rid yourself of...pain, suffering or perhaps something more specific."

"I'm not writing any stupid list! This is all your fault! If you weren't into all the magical mumbo jumbo, none of this would have happened! All I want is to have my daughter back." Molly screams. "We don't have time for this. You have to help me find her! Now!"

Hillary rises and gently embraces her sister and whispers into her ear, "They can be physical symptoms or emotional patterns that affect you and people to whom you are close. Your list grows and you feel whatever emotions arise as you write them down. This is the only way I can think of that might help us find Heidi, Mol."

Molly violently grabs the paper and begins to hit the page with her fist. Her hand splits and as she continues to beat the paper, blood appears and then a word appears— "Dissolution." Finally, Molly is physically spent and sits back on her heels. The two watch in awe as the word magically whirls and gathers other pages until it turns into a magnificent paper tornado. The pages whip sharply and quickly and begin to burrow into the sandy earth floor. Below them, a deep well appears, and reflected on the water, they witness an argument Molly and Steve had just hours before he left to go surfing on that fateful day.

Molly is angrily standing and blocking Steve's way out. "You can't be serious! That woman isn't coming near my daughter if it has anything to do with your hoodoo stuff!"

"My family has a history of untimely deaths. I believe the only way Heidi can be protected is through spiritual intervention. Mol, Heidi is more intuitive than you know. Popo is a Shaman and can train Heidi in the ways of Huna, She needs to learn how to create protective fields by using her own breath and Mana. Popo has lived a long life because she has surrounded herself with protection, and there may be a day when I'm not around."

"So what are you saying, that your family is cursed? That's ridiculous."

"She's ready." Steve locks eyes with Molly. He's not backing down.

"She is too young. I won't allow my daughter to be taught crazy rubbish."

"She's my daughter, too," Steve says, then his tone softens. "Molly, let's not do this now."

"I'll leave and take her with me. That way she'll be protected in California!"

He grabs his bag of surf gear and barely acknowledges Molly's threat with a shake of his head. "No, Molly. You won't." he says and firmly moves Molly aside, the door slamming behind him.

A page flies up from the surface of the water through the well and hits Molly firmly in the chest. When she pulls it away, she cries in horror. It is the legal form she had started to fill out that afternoon, a legal form that, if she had filed it, would have dissolved their marriage.

"I was actually going to leave." Molly clutches the page then throws it into the fire in disgust.

The two women watch the page shrivel up, the smoke curling from the disintegrating fibers and eventually disappearing into the finger-like flames.

Still staring into the flames, Hillary speaks as if in a trance, "This fire has allowed you to release that word. Feel the difference in your body and now, Molly, imagine a scene in which you are free from this word."

The fire dissipates and wisps of smoke curl above tiny glowing embers, both women settle into a peaceful silence.

"He's okay now." Molly looks more relieved that she has since Steve's passing.

"Yes, Moa said so."

"I didn't believe her. And I didn't believe you, either. But now I do."

The second the words are out of Molly's mouth, the walls and fire become a grainy picture and turn into real grass, blue sky and the stone wall. The two are sitting in the deserted park. The pre-dawn dew has settled on their belongings creating a damp cool cover.

"Granddad has the same fear of the unknown that I did. I stuck my head in the sand instead of seeing that my husband was in danger and...Oh,.." Molly struggles to keep her composure. "Granddad said that he would get revenge on Admiral Thomas and his lineage. He's the curse! He killed Steve." Then, as if illuminated by a new resolve, she adds, "Let's save Heidi!"

"Let's try the Huna Prayer again." Hillary sits and pats the ground next to her. "Please."

Molly wipes her tears from her cheek with the back of her hand and slowly sits.

The two calmly breathe Mana and allow their life force energy to wrap ribbons of gorgeous, transformative golden energy around them until dawn arrives.

Just as the sun appears, Granddad rumbles. "You mock me with your willfulness."

"Granddad," Molly voice is steely. "You—and therefore we, by relation—are the reason that there is restricted access to begin with. If the family removes the commitment to 'protect' the portal, everyone who passes on will be free to move at will between the worlds."

Even though he chooses not to show himself, Molly can feel the electric anger surrounding the park. In desperation, she yells, "She's your blood relation, too, Granddad! We know you killed Steve. If you harm her, in any way, you'll be harming another of your own flesh and blood, as well." Molly weeps uncontrollably and pleads, "Please...Oh, God, I beg of you to let her go. I couldn't bear to lose her too."

Then, an eerie silence falls over the park. And Hillary and Molly are held captive while waiting for an answer.

CHAPTER IX

The Promise

Ritual: Heidi's Heart

Oil: Base of Avocado Oil – Frankincense, Myrrh, Cedarwood, Vetiver

Incense: Frankincense

Incantation: "Here I am."

Anoint your chest and wrists as well as the area in which will do this ritual. Find a safe peaceful place where you will remain undisturbed. Burn the Frankincense as you perform this ritual. Sit with eyes closed and legs crossed. Imagine you are in the midst of a battle in a large misty field. See yourself in full armor. Feel the weight of the metal and the heft of a grand sword in your hand. You are ready to face your enemy. You are surrounded by a force field of confidence and it permeates every part of your body, mind and spirit and creates a protective shield. The enemy approaches,

but flees the minute he or she comes close to
your shield and cannot break through.

Move forward in confidence. Know that courage is within you.

✦

A large cold drop of rain hits Hillary on the top of her head. Then another on her arm...the rain begins with enormous drops of water dispersed throughout the park, some fist-sized drops hit the fountain's pool with a ping. The pings increase until the syncopated rhythm builds into an intense cacophony. The downpour creates several small streams, which merge into larger streams that then flow rapidly into the storm drain at the end of the grassy area.

"Over here!" Heidi yells from the opposite end of the park.

When Granddad focused on the immense rainstorm, he left our way out unguarded. So, I seized the opportunity to free Heidi and extracted her from captivity.

"Heidi!" Molly screams and runs toward her daughter, splashing through water and mud.

Hillary runs to Heidi, too and I glide along the side of the wall.

"Mom, it was so cool! I slept on a blanket that was just like Moa's when she was little." Water streams down Heidi's face as she animatedly describes her adventure.

"Let's find shelter first. Then we'll talk." Molly takes her daughter's hand and the three of them run through the sheets of rain toward a group of abandoned shops across the street from the park.

Desperate to find shelter, Hillary pulls on the door-knobs of each shop to no avail. A side door to a former curio shop—the faded sign still hangs above the door—is unlocked and she yells, "In here!" She ushers Molly and Heidi into the musty store and slams the door. They all watch in horror as Granddad unfurls his wrath on Thomas Square Park in the form of a storm of monsoon-like proportions. The banyan trees bend sideways, and one is even uprooted, falling across the park's entry.

I am in my opaque human form so all three of them can see and hear me. "Granddad has achieved some form of release and that means—at least for the moment— the group is safe." I say as I help the women get comfortable while Molly holds Heidi tightly and questions her about her harrowing experience.

"Honest, Mom." Heidi answers, "Moa made sure I was safe."

"Thank you, Moa," Molly says tightly—still unsure of exactly what happened or what to think.

"We still have some more work to do." I've created places for the group to rest for their next journey. "Please know you are safe."

"How do we know we are safe?" Molly is obviously frightened.

"That last, loud burst of thunder was your Granddad sealing the portal with his anger. At least for now, he is gone to a holding place for lost souls. While there, he hears exactly what he wants to hear in order to support his skewed reality. He'll be back, though, because he still wishes to complete his mission regarding the Ancient Portal, but on his own terms. "

"So he cut his nose off to spite his face." Hillary says.

"Exactly." I say.

"I always hated that expression..." Molly smiles slightly, "Remember when dad would declare Cliché Day? Don't throw the baby out with the bathwater. People who throw stones should not live in..."

"...glass houses." Hillary finishes. "Well, that's more of an adage..."

I interrupt this divergence. "It is essential that you three access your individual gifts through a special meditation that I've created."

"Why?" Molly has gotten up and wandered over to the shop door. She turns. "Look, this man may be our relative, he may have caused some trouble, but I will not expose my daughter and myself to any more danger. Now that we are safe, we're going home. Hillary, it's your choice whether you want to come with us or not." Molly takes Heidi by the hand and they walk through the door.

It is raining steadily outside and Heidi pulls her hand away just as Molly puts her hand on the doorknob. "I'm not coming with you, Mom."

"You most certainly are!" Molly grabs Heidi's arm and yanks her toward the door.

"If both Daddy and Granddad are a part of me, I should get to choose what part I play." Heidi plants herself, one hand and leg hugging the doorframe.

"But sweetie, you are a little girl." Molly reasons.

"It doesn't matter. I am brave and that's all that counts. Dad thought I could do it. He said I had more courage than he did when he was my age."

Molly holds on to Heidi and cuddles her close. "I'm not letting you out of my sight until this is over. It isn't safe to leave, because Granddad is still out there. If you stay I stay. We'll go together. After a nice rest everything will seem clearer."

"You sound like Mom. She loved naptime when we were little." Hillary smiles.

As the rain abates, Hillary finds some old tablecloths in a stack and lays them on the dusty floor. They are threadbare, but at least they're clean. Molly spreads them out and the three lie down to nap. Water trickles quietly down the windows and from the trees and Molly hums quietly to soothe her own nerves. Despite the creaks and groans of an unfamiliar place, all three are soon fast asleep.

As soon as the group settles into slumber, they meet in a place between dreams. This is where I took them for their journey with their Granddad—the inner-space. Even though I am currently "homeless" I am able to access this place through their dreams. They are in a long white corridor with many doors.

"As you walk down this hall," I say, "you will each find the key to your heart's desire and in doing so, unlock the gifts of forgiveness and self-love."

As the group begins to walk, Heidi counts the doors they pass. "One…Two…Mom, isn't this exciting?…Three… Four…Five…" She stops, "Hey, see that light green glow up there? I bet that is where we're supposed to go.

When the group reaches the door, they bask in the glow of the intense green light coming from underneath and around the outside of the door.

Hillary turns to the group, and then sees me. "Moa, what are you doing here?"

"Because the portal was closed, I am now able to follow you on your journey." I smile. "While in this vibration, however, I have no extra powers and can merely access the portal. I must experience things as you do."

This time Molly speaks up. "Why do I feel that if we open this door, we will find out some uncomfortable truths about ourselves and, in the process, find out the truth about accepting love in each of our lives?"

"I don't want to go." A look of worry washes over Hillary's face. "I am so ashamed of how I acted toward mom and dad."

"Don't worry, Aunt Hillary," Heidi slips her small hand into Hillary's. "We'll do it together."

Molly reaches out and her heart skips a beat as she turns the doorknob. She slowly opens it to reveal a brightly lit room with green marble walls. The beautiful surroundings radiate a feeling of warmth and protection, and Hillary catches the luscious scent of basil. The room is small and has an inviting round table with eight chairs. There is nothing else in the room.

"It feels like angels are all around us," Heidi quips as they move over to sit in the chairs.

Within seconds of the last of them sitting down, the remaining chairs are occupied with a mirror image of each one.

Hillary, Molly, and Heidi are face to face with themselves!

Heidi pipes up, "Hi there!" Heidi II smiles back and answers with a squealing, "Hello!"

I even have my own carbon copy. Moa II says, "You're not meant to bridge the two worlds. Within one day, you all will be in an entirely new location." Then she addresses the group. "This is your chance to understand what you need to about yourselves with regards to your heart's desire and love. Tell Self-II what is missing and what is wrong. Watch how Self-II receives this information."

"Whoa, that scares me." Molly I and Molly II say at exactly the same time.

"I don't know, I kind of like the idea of going somewhere new." Hillary I smiles at Hillary II.

"After you are finished, Self-II has a gift for you." Moa II says, "This will help you in your quest for answers."

Each double has a blue velvet drawstring bag. She pulls a stone out and gives it to her counterpart.

"What's your stone, Moa?" Heidi curiously eyes Moa II 's empty hands.

Moa II gives me a Nebula Palm Stone and I hold it out for everyone to see. "This stone is for the next leg of your journey. It is formed from and shaped by fire, wind, water and time—all the elements of earth. There is an active regenerative energy embedded within each stone."

"The next leg of your journey." Hillary looks at the group, then at me. "You can't go back! Because you chose to let Granddad go and save Heidi...oh no, Moa...you are stuck on earth! Are you to remain a homeless entity, roaming the earth?"

"Yes." I say calmly. "But, I choose to do so."

"It didn't look like you chose to have Granddad seal the portal," Hillary says.

"Experiences are a part of existence. How we frame them in our minds is a choice. I choose to be here on earth." I say. Smiling, the two Moas merge into one. Each woman receives a warm, loving hug from her other self.

Then the group suddenly reappears back in the confines of the small store. Once back in the shelter of the musty shop, they share their gifts with one another.

"The rain has stopped." Heidi opens her hand to reveal a beautifully tumbled red jasper stone. "I asked for protection and my double told me red jasper is the oldest known gemstone and will keep me safe and bring luck."

Hillary shows the group a blue chalcedony three-dimensional star. "I asked how I could help Moa get home. It is the sacred geometric shape called Obsidian Merkaba—a channel of divine light. Chalcedony absorbs negative energy and dissipates it and assists in telepathy. Oh, and it instills generosity."

Heidi and Hillary look at Molly, who has tears streaming down her face. "An audible gasp runs through the group as she opens her hand to reveal an amethyst angel. "I asked why Steve was taken so soon. My double told me that he has work to do on the other side and that she brought a sliver of his spirit and placed it here." Molly points to the angel's wings.

The three women hold each other and weep until they are dry. Heidi is the first to pull away. "Where's Moa?" she sniffs.

Emerging from the store, they find Thomas Square in an upheaval after the storm. Hillary, Molly and Heidi stand silently taking in the destruction. Limbs and leaves litter the ground. Leaves, trash and signs have all been washed into the storm drain. The fountain is filled to the brim with crystal clear water.

Heidi is the first to speak. "Holy cow! I guess the rain washed all the muck out of the fountain."

Thankfully, Molly and Heidi's house as well as the rest of the city has remained untouched by the tremendous storm.

As the sun emerges between cracks of thick white clouds, the women wander back home in a daze.

"I'm sure Moa will be fine." Hillary says.

"How do you know that she'll be okay?" Heidi asks.

"Sometimes you have to speak your wishes out loud to make them come true." Hillary says wearily. She is secretly worried that she'll never see me again.

The group returns home, and immediately they all head for the kitchen.

"I'm starved," Molly says.

"Me, too," Heidi adds.

They pull together a wonderful dinner of rice and Nori, miso soup and Huli Huli chicken. Molly makes the chicken's sauce by simmering pineapple juice, ginger and a little shoyu until it thickens. The result is an intense tasty sweet-and-spicy mixture.

The group settles down in the breakfast nook and eats in silence. The day's events buzz in their heads.

"What do you think Moa will do now?" Hillary finally asks what Heidi and Molly have been thinking.

"I imagine she'll have to find another job." Heidi says pensively.

"I wonder what jobs are open for a newly integrated entity with gate keeping experience?"

The food is finished, dishes done and no one wants to sleep. They wander out to the lanai and relax into the cushioned wicker recliners to loll in the shade. Before Heidi succumbs to slumber, she raises her head from her mother's lap and sleepily mumbles, "I didn't get to say goodbye."

"I'm really worried about Moa." Hillary says.

"Remember what you said, Hil. Your wish will come true if you believe it. She'll be fine." Molly says sleepily.

Hillary sits alone in an oversized wicker chair. Her feet are propped up and she peruses the treetops for any unusual movement. There is no Moa, as far as she can see—just gorgeous orange and yellow hued dusk sky and surrounding greenery. Breathing deeply, she drifts into a twilight sleep. And just as in her previous experiences, she finds herself in a new inner-space.

"Another door." Hillary says to no one.

She can sense Heidi and Molly still asleep as well as herself, but she is alone in this new place. It's almost like she is experiencing the phenomena that I explained. She is on two tuners at the same time. One location is in Molly's house and the other is somewhere else. In front of her is a door and she decides to enter. There are two comfortable chairs sitting one in front of the other. She sits down and sees herself in the chair—Self-II—this time, however, Self-II is wearing a deep blue robe.

"Hello, Hillary." Self-II says, "You may confess any and all wrongs, ills, upsets, anger, health problems, and anything else that you desire. By speaking your truth," Self-II says, "you will create a new vibration within your fifth chakra—the energy center within your body that governs your voice. This healing vibration will shatter all previous blocks and discomfort."

"I wish I was a better daughter. In all my work to, essentially, create my own practice, I hurt my parents. I spoke harshly to them and walked away."

Hillary watches as Self-II compassionately receives the information and waits for more. She relaxes and begins to express other regrets, hurts, misunderstandings and sins, Self-II sits calmly, gracefully and open.

She is not sure how much time has passed, however, after her last bit of regret has been expelled, Self-II reaches out to place a hand over Hillary's throat, and she feels a new energy entering her body.

"What's happening to me?" Hillary says quietly.

"I am recalibrating the vibration of your fifth chakra."

Hillary rises to leave and Self-II gives her a warm hug. She receives this love deeply and thanks Self-II for all of her help and understanding.

She awakens the next morning with a new quiet resolve. Grabbing the blue chalcedony star Hillary says aloud, "With the 24 hours I have left, I'm going to help Moa find a way home."

CHAPTER X

Caution

Ritual: Self-Trust
Oil: Base of Grapeseed Oil – Nutmeg, Marjoram,
Cypress Incense: Sweet Grass
Incantation: "My aims are pure and my intentions are good. I trust my intuition."

Sit alone in a room where you will remain undisturbed. Burn the sweet grass and repeat the incantation. Hear the words and let the vibration echo through your body. If you feel they do not resonate through a certain body part, send healing light until the part is cleared.

We are born with certain instincts and we may be taught to deny them, depending on our family situation. You are always free to choose to believe in yourself and trust your instincts.

Hillary is intent on helping me on the next leg of my journey. She decides to head out to Thomas Square Park to inspect the damage and quickly scribbles a note—*Gone to park to find Moa*—-to Molly. Perhaps, she reasons, I am either there or she will find a clue about where I might have gone.

The scene at Thomas Square Park is astounding. Yellow police caution tape surrounds the once majestic park. Although the largest and oldest banyan tree is still standing, the youngest did not fare as well. Thick tree roots dangle pieces of sandy sod, blocking the area that was once the entrance to the park. Hillary sits on a low wall just outside the tape and waits.

But, I don't come.

She moves to a section next to the, now, clear-flowing fountain in the middle of the park and performs the Huna Prayer.

And still, no sign of me.

After three hours of sitting in the heat, she is dripping with sweat and decides to go back to the house. Perhaps Molly or Heidi has some information to add.

However, when Hillary returns, she finds Molly and Heidi have gone and left her a note:

Meet us at the boardwalk at Waikiki near the bike stand.

Hillary knows where the bike stand is. On a previous trip, Molly, Hillary, Heidi and Steve had taken a glorious bike ride along a strip on the west side of the island. They'd even spotted a school of dolphin frolicking in the sparkling surf. The bike stand is a fair distance from the apartment, but still walkable. So, after a quick change of clothes, Hillary sets out to find her sister and niece.

As she walks, a slight buzzing begins in her ears, which increases with every step. Finally, she has to stop and regather her thoughts and energy. Is it the heat? A blood sugar thing? Fallout from the otherworldly journeys she's been taking?

    She stops at a convenience store to buy some cold water, the female clerk giving her a perfunctory nod as she hands Hillary her change. Hillary gulps the cool refreshing water as she sits on the stoop next door. Although the water helps, the buzzing in her ear increases; still, she travels on, despite the discomfort. Finally, Hillary reaches the bike stand and peruses the beach. Tourists are all around enjoying the afternoon sun and beach activities.

A nearby stand offers Shave Ice, and Hillary looks around for her sister and niece but they are nowhere to be found.

She gets a strawberry Shave Ice, finds a prime spot on a bench in the shade and settles in to wait. Surely they will be along soon. Together, the heat and long walk lull her into a daze and before she knows it, she is sitting on a large indigo colored cushion. She feels a sense of calm just by sitting on this cushion. As she settles further into this comfortable and peaceful position, she senses the presence of another person sitting across from her. The more she calms down, the more clearly this other form comes into focus. It's Hillary's Self-II sitting across from her on another indigo colored cushion.

There is a large opaque veil between Hillary and her double. Hillary is overwhelmed with happiness to see Self-II, however, before she can give a hug, Hillary notices that an image of her sleeping body—still on the park bench—is being projected onto the veil.

"This is you, right now. You are asleep on the park bench." Self-II says. "I will switch the tuner and voila—you are back at high school.

Hillary watches a particularly painful incident with a popular boy, Chad Murphy, from her school.

It's the afternoon of the first day of junior year and Chad limps over to Hillary and her group of friends. He is tall, muscular and favors his right leg—an injury from the last summer scrimmage game.

"Hi Hillary. Can I talk with you for a second over here?" Hillary is shocked that Chad knows her name. He has dated two of the three "Threats"—Brenda Stone missed that boat when she scratched her initials into the girls bathroom stall—BS+CM=LV—and was caught and immediately expelled. Although he is friendly with almost everyone at their school, the exception has been the "Mush." Its not that he has been unfriendly, more like he is completely oblivious to their daily adoration. But, with this conversation, that all seems to be changing. Nonetheless, he motions to a bench a few feet away.

When they are just out of earshot, they sit. Chad's hazel eyes pierce Hillary's soul. "I was wondering if you are free this weekend."

She digs her toe into a weed-filled crack and unearths a stone. "Um, why?" Hillary is free this weekend and the one after that and the one after, as well, but she can't imagine why—after two years of high school Chad Murphy would suddenly ask this question.

"I saw you in history class and everyone knows you're a genius. Could you, um...tutor me?" Chad smells like fresh geraniums and Hillary feels like she'll float away on his fragrant presence at any moment. He rises. "Come on, I'll give you a ride home and we can talk." Upon seeing Hillary look at her friends Chad says, "They'll be fine. Come on." He begins to walk in toward the parking lot, then looks back at her. Hillary stays seated until Chad gives her an irreverent upward "guy nod"—a movement reserved for cocky boys and smug jocks. She takes the bait and follows his sharp spicy scent to his gorgeous new yellow Mustang convertible.

Hillary's heart leaps as she hops into his car and is enveloped in 'new car smell.' Her parents could never afford to give her anything so expensive. And, Hillary suspects, even if they could, her father would make her earn it. Hillary is positive that Chad has never had to earn anything in his life. He starts the car, the engine rumbles and Chad leans over and gives Hillary a luscious, toe curling, passionate kiss. It is the third kiss she has received from a boy.

The first was a doughy kiss laid upon her at a seventh grade dance from Joey Sharp who had just eaten a mouthful of pretzels. The second was with Brady Mann during freshman year and occurred on a group date to the movies, when he planted a rum and Coke kiss on her during the film and then ended their date with a fist bump. This kiss tops both of those others and leaves her floating as Chad pulls out of the school parking lot.

Although Chad is a careful driver, Hillary's pulse continues to pound as they cruise through the town. She can still feel his lips on hers, his hot breath on her neck. And she can barely keep up with the surface banter. However, the conversation takes an abrupt turn when he begins to outline a plan to get answers for the midterm history test.

"No," Hillary doesn't even hesitate with her answer. "Cheating doesn't work for me."

Upon hearing her answer, Chad jerks the wheel, careening across two lanes of traffic, pulls up to the sidewalk and says through gritted teeth, "Get Out."

Hillary walks the rest of the way home. Kicking herself for ever believing that anyone who associates the "Threats" could be civil. But, she is pleased with herself for not giving in to his ridiculous request.

What she hadn't planned on was Chad's retaliatory actions. The next day when Hillary enters her school, she is met with secretive stares and tittering whispers from some unlikely people—"The Mushketeers."

None of her friends will even give her an explanation until she corners her friend Sarah, after first period, "What happened? He's telling everyone that you kissed him and when he rejected you, you put a spell on him so next time he plays football he'll get another injury." Then Sarah shifts uncomfortably and whispers, "He told everyone that we are a coven and you are our leader. Hillary, we can't have people thinking we are a bunch of witches. It's one thing to have people guess, but it's another to have a popular guy telling first-hand experience."

Although Hillary tried to explain what happened and she remained friends with "The Mush," after that things were never quite the same.

Self-II points out, as the scene plays out that Hillary's hurt feelings still exist, but are going on in another frequency.

Then Self-II switches back to the first frequency in which Hillary is sleeping on the bench. "Would you like to change your behavior that day?" Self-II places a hand on the center of her forehead.

"This is your Sixth chakra and directs clearing indigo energy into your Third Eye." Self-II explains.

Hillary can feel a slight buzzing through her head—very similar to the buzzing that occurred as she was walking to meet Molly and Heidi. Then, Self-II changes the tuner on the veil between them and replays the scene with Hillary in a different role. Instead of caving into the pressures of being popular, she asks Chad more questions and finds out very quickly about his motives to cheat. This time, she tells him to take a flying leap.

As Hillary watches the new scene, Self-II tells her how she may change her current situation as easy as changing a television tuner. "The only difference is the vibrational frequency or the attitude with which you view the issue. This attitude is a lens, which defines your life and by watching yourself and your behavior, wishing to change that behavior and modifying the lens through which you view that challenge, change is possible."

Hillary asks Self-II what she can do about Moa. The word "choice" materializes on the veil.

"But what does that mean!" Hillary is exasperated.

"It means that your free will is a gift and now is the time to exercise it to its full capacity." says Self-II. "Hillary, you may return here with me to transform anything else that is bothering you whenever you wish."

Hillary thanks Self-II and closes her eyes as she comes back from this magnificent experience. She is filled with a sense of peaceful knowing, a feeling of centered calm, and best of all her head has stopped buzzing and she feels clear and focused.

She is jolted from her meditation experience by Heidi. "Aunt Hillary, you missed it!"

Hillary shakes off the daze and watches as her niece dances excitedly around.

"We saw an Anuenue!" Heidi cheers.

"An actual rainbow or the people who are Anuenue?" Hillary asks.

"A man," Molly chimes in, "It was amazing, Hillary."

"He was so tall and friendly..." Heidi begins. "And he and mommy had coffee."

"They did?" Hillary raises her eyebrows.

"Yes, and he said that Moa was going to be reassigned to another portal. She'll be fine."

Hillary gets a strange and uncomfortable feeling, but keeps it to herself as Heidi continues, "And he said that now that the portal is gone, that area is a lot safer. He said he'd take us to Moa, too."

"I was skeptical at first," Molly leans in close to Hillary as Heidi skips over to a group of girls her age. "But this guy was pretty convincing. He told us to meet him at Hoki Burger."

"I don't know, Molly." Hillary shifts uncomfortably, "It doesn't feel right to me."

"Didn't you spend the entire morning waiting for Moa at the Park? She helped us, this is our chance to help her."

Molly walks over, grabs Heidi's hand, turns back and looks at Hillary.

"Okay." Hillary catches up and they make their way down the crowded sidewalk to the front of Hoki Burger. The building is decorated with thick wooden cutouts of fish painted in bright colors. Heidi runs her fingers over a yellow and pink finned tuna.

"Hello, Hillary." A dark haired man approaches. He is tall—about a foot taller than the surrounding pedestrians. Hillary guesses he used to play basketball. "I'm Paul."

Hillary extends her hand and they shake, "Hi, Paul. I understand you can help us find Moa." His warm smile and kind demeanor quell Hillary's fears.

"Yes. Follow me." He lopes ahead and calls behind. "She's safe, but needs to recharge after the incident with your Granddad."

"You know about that?" Hillary runs ahead and catches up with him leaving Molly and Heidi further behind.

"Sure." Paul says nothing for the rest of the walk, which soon turns into a trek. The sidewalk ends and they hike in the sand along the water's edge.

Just as Hillary is about to ask for a water stop, Paul turns in to a lush alcove of trees. Hillary stops, unsure that she wants to go any further. She catches Molly's arm, "Mol, I don't think its safe."

Paul stops and speaks calmly, "Look behind you, you'll see that there is nowhere to go but in here."

"Oh, no." Molly gasps.

Much to their horror, they turn and see that the tide has come in and completely blocked their way home!

"That's okay." Hillary says. "I have a plan." The three walk single file with Hillary in the rear and Molly in the front. Brave Heidi is holding it together well. Although

111

thorny gorse bushes line the path, no one in the group catches her legs or arms.

Paul disappears around a curve in the trail. The group has reached a glen surrounded by stony mountains. Behind them is the thorny trail and in front of them are tall sheer faces of rock.

"We're lost!" cries Heidi.

"I think we should turn back." Molly says. "Surely there's another way out of here."

"Or we could go up there." Heidi points to a glowing ladder in front of them that extends up the face of rock and extends into a misty cloud.

She walks over and runs her hand over a rung. The material is solid to the touch, however it appears to be made of pure white light. She looks back at Molly, "I'll go up and investigate and you both stay here."

She lifts her foot onto the first rung. It is solid enough to stand on and seems to hold her weight. As she begins climbing, she gets the sense that this ladder leads to a divine energy. Apparently, Molly and Heidi get the same feeling because Hillary looks down to see Heidi, then Molly coming up, too.

"Somehow I feel that by going up this ladder, we will attain access to our highest wisdom and intelligence." Molly yells up to Hillary. "You'll be fine."

"Didn't you say that about Moa?" Hillary laughs, "And we can't find her anywhere!"

"It feels like angel energy..." Heidi says excitedly.

CHAPTER XI

Rainbow's End

Ritual: Angelic Guidance
Oil: Base of Coconut Oil – Neroli, Lavender,
Chamomile Incense: Lavender
Incantation: "I am in the Light and of the Light."

Burn the lavender and allow the smoke to drift around your head. Anoint the top of your head, your third eye and the bottom of your feet. Sit calmly and repeat the incantation. As you do so, imagine a beautiful golden light descends from the heavens and covers your entire body with warmth and love. This light is joy. It also brings knowledge and soul messages. Listen carefully and you may hear them. Sit quietly for as long as needed and repeat often to gain angelic protection and guidance.

If you ask for guidance, it is heard. Wait for the answer. Know that you are never alone.

⸸

Hillary steps off the ladder first and shields her face from the intense light. Blinking until her eyes acclimate to the radiantly illuminated space, she is greeted by a beautiful woman with long dark brown hair. The light emanates from this luminous woman who is dressed in a flowing silver robe. She smiles at Hillary warmly.

"Hi Hillary, I'm Chandara your angelic guide."

Heidi's guide, Wellesley, helps her up off the ladder and Catherine greets Molly as she walks toward the group. Wellesley is the largest of the guides with enormous opalescent wings. She explains that she is a Seraph. Angelic guides are often of different stages or levels—Molly and Hillary's guides are Cherubim, the next level below the Seraphim on the Angelic Hierarchy. Wellesley explains that Seraphim are the highest in the Angelic order.

"We hold the divine fire, love and the unshielded light of God." Wellsley's voice comes through clearly, although her lips don't move.

"Our power lies within the cosmic realm including the sun, moon and stars," Chandara adds.

"We were led here by Paul, an Anuenue." Hillary has finally gotten her bearings in the extremely bright location. "Where did he go?"

"He was about to hand you over to the Anuenue sect for the crime of destroying their livelihood." Catherine moves close to Molly and, curiosity getting the best of her, begins to touch Molly's hair.

"What does 'destroying their livelihood' mean?" The touch so unnerves Molly, she scoots closer to Wellesley.

"You'll have to excuse Catherine, she has never been human and this is only her second assignment with earthly beings." Wellesley says kindly. "If Moa no longer works as a Gatekeeper for the Ancients and everyone who passes on is allowed to freely move through the Ancient portal, then the Anuenue will no longer be needed on earth to translate and escort humans through the portal. The Anuenue feel that if they no longer have this job, then their very existence is threatened. We sent the ladder to you as an escape and your ability to have faith, even in the face of harm, brought you here."

"When you have faith, you believe that a power bigger than yourself exists. We are that unshielded power of the divine. Please sit while we give you the sustenance you need." Wellesley motions to three comfortable chairs. As the three sit, an Angel dressed in blue gives them cool water and wafts blue energy over each of them.

After each has received comfort and care, an Archangel with gilded wings and a gossamer robe reads from a scroll in her elegant outstretched arms, "The guide has access to knowledge beyond your comprehension so after you ask, know that the message you receive will be perfect for your circumstances and will come in a way that you fully understand."

"Heidi, Molly and Hillary, your bravery is valued on this side. These gifts are connected to your lineage in the form of healing. Your family, in both heaven and earth is grateful for your help and wishes to bestow an honorific of Celestial Earth Guide to you." The Archangel places a beautiful crown of stars around each of their heads.

They rise and bow in gratitude for their gifts. When the Archangel is finished, she calls Wellesley, Catherine and Chandara over. The Angelic Guides then place their hands above Hillary, Heidi and Molly's crown chakra and send a vibrating white light into their bodies creating an amazing glow of light energy and a sense of joy and well being.

As the Angelic Guides perform this light treatment, Wellesley says, "This profound energy fills any dark and empty places and neutralizes any remaining negativity."

Then, each of them is given a pair of opalescent wings. Heidi's are the same size as Hillary and Molly.

They rise and thank their Angelic Guides for their help and healing guidance. "Even though these wings cannot be seen by humans and cannot help you physically fly, they will always remain with you and assist you to return here whenever you wish." Catherine says gently.

"Before you leave, there is one more gift. It was granted on behalf of your friend Moa and is right over here." Wellesley motions to an area that—even in this bright space—makes Molly, Heidi and Hillary squint.

As their eyes adjust, a male form within a large opalescent bubble shimmers in the distance. The bubble floats toward the group and finally comes to rest in front of them, then explodes with a resounding pop.

"Daddy." Heidi screams and throws herself on Steve's shimmering body.

Molly is instantly by his side and buries her nose in his neck. Hillary allows them time as she sniffles and wipes her eyes with the back of her hand.

Words pour out of Heidi as fast as Molly's tears come, "Oh, we didn't get to say goodbye but now you're here and I love you so much. Where were you? Can you stay? I love you Daddy? Do you live with the angels? They are wonderful!"

"I love you," he says into Molly's hair.

Molly breathes in his scent trying to hold it within her as long as she can.

"My keiki," Steve says to Heidi.

She takes her father's large hand and cradles it between her neck and shoulder.

Hillary slowly walks over to the group and Steve extends an arm to pull her in to the familial embrace.

"Mahalo, Hillary, for bringing Moa, and therefore, Molly and Heidi for a meeting in this angelic realm."

"My pleasure." Hillary is still holding on to Steve and doesn't want to let go.

Wellesley catches Steve's eye and he nods. "I must go," he says. "I cannot return to earth with you, but I am so grateful for this chance to say 'aloha.'"

The group steps away, and just before he is again enveloped by the opalescent bubble, Heidi says bravely, "Goodbye, Daddy."

Steve floats away with the beautiful sparkling orb and Heidi keeps her tiny hand up in a wave long after he has disappeared into the Light.

"You may go with eternal peace and blessed understanding." Catherine calls to them as they descend the light ladder.

When Hillary reaches the base of the ladder, she finds that she is on the shore, the sun has set, a full moon is rising on the ocean's horizon and the tide has gone out. The group is free to go home and they do so in haste.

"I hope Moa's okay." Heidi says as she skips up the front steps to her home.

"Don't worry, Heidi, I believe I have the answer to our questions." Hillary is on her heels and ready for bed.

They put on pajamas, brush teeth and tumble in bed grateful to be home. Just before she turns out her bedside light, Hillary smiles to herself. She has wings!

Hillary sets her alarm for 5:30 am and, for the first time in three days, is able to sleep through the night undisturbed. She dreams of using her newly acquired angel wings to soar over Hawaii. She passes over Diamond Head, curves around the North Shore and glides effortlessly a few feet above the glittering ocean.

When she wakes, the sun is just peeking through her window. Hillary takes a shower and dresses in the beautiful long verdant patterned muumuu she wore on the first day she visited Thomas Square Park. After finishing, she stands in front of her box of oils. None of them seem appropriate at this point. After all the angel wings and chakra clearings, the oils didn't seem needed. Since she is not sure that she'll connect with Moa, she'll have to assume that she'll battle the Anuenue alone.

Heidi comes down the stairs in her most intriguing outfit yet. She's sporting a tank top covered in brightly-colored gems and a gauze skirt with multi-layers of iridescent colors.

"I love it!" Hillary hugs her niece and buries her nose in her sweet smelling hair. They walk into the kitchen together.

Molly greets the two in the kitchen with a lovely breakfast of huevos rancheros, eggs over easy on a bed of corn tortillas with shredded Monterey Jack cheese and pico de gallo on top.

She hands Hillary a steaming cup of Kona coffee and smiles. "I know you don't normally drink coffee, but it looks like you'll need all the strength you can get. Ready to face the Anuenue?"

"Yes. I've got 8 hours and absolutely no plan, but I think that is how it needs to be. The Hekili are able to read thoughts, so it is best to act in the present."

"I still don't understand why the Hekili are so upset, Auntie."

"Because they no longer have the power they used to, and must find new ways to exist. The challenge will be discerning the good from the bad Anuenue. Some Anuenue consider themselves superior beings and do not use the name Hekili."

Hillary receives a loving hug and kiss from both Heidi and Molly, and then grabs her shoulder bag. She has made sure to stock her bag with her magical tools—the wand, crystal ball—and walks off to gather the additional items she'll need to defeat the Anuenue.

She begins her journey by walking to the ocean and gathering a travel-sized container full of water and one of sand. On the way, she stops off to get a large bottle of water at a Quick Mart. At the check out stand, the woman ringing her up—a tiny dark haired woman—asks if she'd like any gum or sunglasses. Hillary declines the offer and hands the woman cash. However, the woman reaches under the counter and places a pair of bright pink, green and purple shades into the bag with the water. The sunglasses are made of thick plastic and, although sturdy, they are a mishmash of neon colors—Hillary would never wear eyewear this gaudy.

Annoyed Hillary pulls them out and places them back on the counter, "Excuse me, as you can plainly see from the sunglasses on my face, I do not need another pair."

"Trust me, Hillary. Today, of all days, you'll need them." The woman holds them out.

Shocked that this stranger knows her first name, Hillary takes the glasses from the smiling woman, places them inside her bag and walks quickly out of the store.

Shaking off the absurdity, Hillary continues to walk toward City Hall to cut some bitter orange leaves. Pettigrain, an essential oil made from bitter orange tree leaves is used in purification rites. Perhaps, Hillary reasons, there are some unseen blocks within her that could potentially be keeping her from finding Moa. By clearing her mind, body and spirit, she may be able to find Moa more easily.

The City Hall building is lined with bitter orange bushes and Hillary takes out a small pair of scissors—borrowed from her sister—and snips three sprigs. As she shoves the clippings in her bag, the back of her neck tingles.

"Excuse me, miss. It is illegal to take any indigenous plants from State owned property."

Hillary whirls around, about to defend her actions when she erupts into peels of laughter, "MOA!"

I stand on the warm sidewalk, and look just as I did when I escaped into the portal—a 7 year old girl, my soft kapa cloth dress fluttering in the breeze, my long brown-black hair blows into my eyes and I tuck it behind my ear.

"You're...you're real." Hillary is elated to have me back and gives me a long hug. It feels wonderful. She pulls away and looks deep into my eyes, "Where have you been?"

"Oh, here and there..." I say with a mysterious smile, "... and everywhere."

"What happened to you?" She kneels down beside me.

"Actually, I met with the Light Consortium and the only way I could come back and help you was in human form..."

"They allowed that?"

"It is highly unusual for the Ancient elders to endorse such an unorthodox method of work, however, I convinced them."

"How does it feel?" Hillary puts her arm around me.

"I don't know. It's difficult to find words...stup..." I hesitate, searching for the perfect word.

"Stupid?" Hillary looks concerned.

"Well, I was going to say 'stupendous' but, now I'll add glorious...and a little weird." Then, I smile and put my arm around her, too. "In any case, we have to work together in a new way to defeat the Hekili."

"I've got the sea water, sand and bitter orange cuttings. Is there anything else?" Hillary opens her bag to reveal the items.

"Looks good to me." I say.

Then Hillary and I make our way to Thomas Square Park. The banyan trees shiver in the noon breeze. A group of students from the Art Academy across the street is milling around, taking pictures of the majestic banyans. For a moment, it appears as if the banyans are stretching, preening and posing proudly. A blonde, petite girl holds an expensive camera and positions herself on the exact spot where the Portal once stood.

"Is that dangerous?" Hillary whispers to me.

"I don't think so." I say, "How can you fall into something that has been sealed up tight.

"Still," Hillary replies, "It doesn't seem like the safest place to be located—given the circumstances. See any Anuenue around?"

"I don't know what they look like from a human perspective." I shrug. "Looks like we'll have to rely on our five senses."

The girl delicately bends down to tie her shoe and Hillary approaches her and hovers in the girl's periphery.

"Pardon. Do you mind moving so I can get a picture of this area?"

"Yes." The girls face is turned away, so Hillary is sure she does not hear her correctly.

"What did you say?"

"Yes. I mind." The girl looks up and her face seems changed. Her pupils are almost as big as her irises and she steels herself, verbally poking Hillary, "I'm not moving."

A flinch tells me she is about to strike out, so I yell, "Hillary, she's an Anuenue! Watch out!"

The girl tries to grab Hillary by the hair, but instead trips on a tree root. None of the others at the park notice. I manage to escape and hide behind the stone wall. Dust flies as the Hekili—in the form of a petite student—falls face first into a dry bush with a loud grunt. Hillary's sunglasses fly off her face in the scuffle and she loses her bag containing the seawater, sand and bitter orange. The plastic bag, however, with the water and gaudy sunglasses still swings around her wrist.

The girl staggers from the bush with fury clouding her face. She screams and charges after Hillary. "You did that on purpose."

The chase ensues. Hillary deftly crosses a busy intersection the bag banging against her side. I run after the two—still not sure of how I can help Hillary, but wanting to be near, just in case I am able to do so. An angry man in a blue sedan honks and opens his door in an attempt to yell at Hillary, but instead blocks the girl's path. With a thud, the girl crashes into the door head first and other motorists exit their cars to help her up. Hillary ducks under a woman's outstretched arms and weaves between the cock-eyed cars looking for a way past the mess and away from the fray.

I continue to run past the melee and yell, "Keep going. I'll catch up with you."

Hillary escapes around the corner and continues to run for three more blocks. Once behind a building, she rests.

I catch up to Hillary. "Great work! You managed to evade an Hekili."

Huffing, Hillary nods, and pulls out the water and takes a few gulps. She finishes the bottle quickly, throws it with the bag into a nearby recycle bin. She considers throwing the sunglasses in, too, but thinking twice, keeps them in her hand.

"How are you not out of breath?" She shakes her head.

"I don't know. Probably genetic." I smile. "Let's go back and find the Hekili and see what she wants."

"Are you insane?" She wipes the sweat off her face with the side of her dress and squints. "I can't tell who the Anuenue are and I'm surely not going to put myself in that position again. Plus, all the items I collected are back at the park."

The noontime glare gets the better of her and Hillary slips the sunglasses on.

"Here's a bonus," she says, "if I wear them, I don't have to look at them."

Then, she heads toward her sister's house. "You can go back to being an entity and I can continue on my vacation!" Hillary tries to find the shade as she walks. It's a losing battle.

"Ugh, it's hot! Isn't there anyone we can trust, Moa?"

"No. All the Anuenue have the potential for corruption." I say.

"There has to be a way to tell the diff..." Hillary halts mid-sentence. Staring straight ahead, her mouth gapes. "The shirt."

"What?" I say.

"The shirt from the airplane." She whispers. "I saw some-one..." A man passes us and she nods stiffly then continues, "with that same exact shirt on my incoming flight."

125

"So?"

"I guess you're right." She softens. "Probably just a coincid....ACH!" She ducks behind a tree and pulls me with her. "Oh, Moa, you're not going to believe this!"

She hands me the drug store sunglasses and I suddenly see what has so alarmed Hillary. Hundreds of people peppered through the parks, walking in and out of businesses, riding bikes and all of them wearing bright orange, purple and green stripes!

"I think the store clerk gave you the glasses so you could see the Anuenue who are wearing those ridiculously loud shirts!"

"Oh, Moa, this is incredible!" Hillary takes the glasses back to get a better look.

A mother wears the shirt while pushing a baby stroller. A surfer rides by with one on, too. Hillary removes the glasses and the mother is actually wearing tan shorts and a sleeveless light blue shirt. The surfer wears a wet suit.

"Amazing!" I say. "Your guides showed you the shirt on the plane as a way to identify it now."

"I didn't speak to anyone on the plane." Hillary says.

"Guides can come in many forms. The ones that showed you the shirt were there to protect you and existed in a vibration that you could not see."

"Let's go back to the store where the lady gave me the sunglasses." Hillary says. "She might have some ideas about how to defeat the Anuenue."

We skip along, taking turns with the glasses and share our observations. I notice that Anuenue are adults, and Hillary sees a male buy an Anuenue shirt from an open-air fruit stand. The proprietor removes the shirt from a stack sitting out in plain view. When she removes the glasses, it appears as if he is buying a watermelon. The stack of shirts is actually a stack of bags.

Back at the convenience store the clerk is hard at work. I bypass the line and clear my throat, "Ahem, excuse me, ma'am."

"Bathroom not for customah!" She yells.

Hillary jumps in, "But we don't..."

"Go next door to china shop. Bathroom in back!" The clerk continues to scan the items without looking up.

I start to speak, but the woman utters something in Korean and points a bony finger out the door.

"Well, that didn't go as planned." Hillary says as we walk out the door.

To the left is a bike shop, and its doors are locked and gated. To the right is a dingy, second hand store. Its front window advertises "China Shop" in chipped gilded letters.

"Actually, I do have to go to the bathroom." I say.

"So do I," Hillary agrees.

A bell jingles as we open the creaking and swollen wood door of the china shop. Not a soul is around.

"Hello?" Hillary calls out expectantly.

"She said the bathroom was in back." I say. "Let's go."

The shop has no air conditioning and we see a filthy door at the far end of the narrow dusty shop. A tiny sign above says "Restroom."

I flip on the light—a single bare bulb suspended by a wire from the yellowing, peeling ceiling. The mirror is smeared and clouded over as if cleaned by a far-sighted well meaning person. And there is a faint smell of mothballs mixed with spearmint in the stagnant air.

The commode is clean-ish and the small square tile floor looks as if it has been mopped with a broom—dirt moved around in evenly lined swirls. The result is not totally disgusting, but makes us want to leave as quickly as we can.

When we are done, we wander through the dusty aisles. A voice surprises us both. "You like?"

A frail old man stands with a cane. His white hair and slight features make him look unusually old. On earth there are "old souls," people who have lived lifetime upon lifetime on earth and carry their experiences with them not only in their body, but also in their soul. This is a man who radiates ancient "old soul" wisdom on every level—body, mind and soul.

"You come!" He says matter-of-factly.

"It can't hurt." Hillary mumbles to me. And we both trail slowly behind.

He opens the door to a dimly lit, cool room. There is one window and a small lamp opposite. It looks like this is his one room apartment. A well-worn love seat covered in lace doilies is on one wall and two folding chairs are on another.

All is quiet.

"You safe for journey." The man says and closes the door. A second later, we hear a dead bolt fall shut.

We're locked in!

CHAPTER XII

A New Job

Ritual: Balance
Oil: Base of Almond Oil – Angelica, Myrtle,
Patchouli Incense: Sage
Incantation: "Om."

Light the sage and clear the area in which you will perform this ritual. Anoint your third eye and crown with the oil. Lie quietly. Inhale and exhale three times, then imagine the color red surrounding you. Breathe in the color red. Exhale and say the incantation, as you release any feelings or physical discomforts that arise. Do the same with each of the following colors in this order: orange, yellow, green, blue, indigo and white. Relax and breathe in balanced, calming energy.

Healing is accessible from within.
Know you are balanced and safe.

✛

"This isn't good." Hillary tries the door and finds that it is, indeed, locked from the outside.

"Wait." I say. "He told us we are safe for our journey. I know how we can defeat the Anuenue!"

"But you are in human form. Do you still have any of your extraordinary powers?" Hillary looks tense.

"Human's have infinite power within to create healing. The first step is trusting that this power exists. Let's sit here on the floor."

We sit on the ground. I pull a green, orange and navy crocheted blanket from the chair and I put it around Hillary's shoulders.

"Close your eyes." I say. And I imagine that I create a crystal bubble around Hillary and myself with my unique version of Mana—human breath or chi energy—Peko. This charged area begins to pulsate with light energy.

I'm unsure about which powers I can still access as a human and I am pleased to see that I can connect with the Peko energy. This will allow me to bring in a protective field as well as center me in my new body.

"This is incredible, I can feel a cord starting at my tailbone, which leads deep into the earth!"

"Yes, that cord draws in grounding, earth energy. Feel the lower half of your body becoming solid, strong and stable with this energy. By clearing the energy points in our bodies, we can find a way to defeat the Anuenue."

"But what do our chakras have to do with the Anuenue?" Hillary's eyes are still closed, but she is skeptical.

"They control humans by creating fear. To do so, they connect with emotions by tuning in to our chakras and create imbalance—which supports and nourishes fear."

"So, if we clear and protect each chakra we can conquer our fears and can no longer be manipulated by the Anuenue." Hillary says.

"Yes! But, we have to work together." I say, "Are you ready?"

"Sure." Hillary reluctantly says.

"Now focus on your First chakra." I say, "This is the point at the base of your spine between your back and front. What does it look like?"

"I can't see anything. My eyes are closed." Hillary says.

"This is an 'inner sight.' Sort of like picturing an event that has already passed, or trying to imagine what your sister and Molly are doing right now. It's your 'mind's eye.' Ideally, each chakra should be a clockwise spinning ball of clear red energy. If there are any dark spots on your chakra or it looks or feels like it is unusually large or small, slow or fast, send a beam of healing white light and hear the mantra "LAM" directly into the First chakra to clear and vibrate any darkness or sluggishness away. Continue to send the white light energy until you see and feel your First chakra spinning clockwise and bright red. Breathe in secure, calm and centering red energy."

"I see it, Moa." Hillary says excitedly.

"You see an elevator door, right?"

"Yes. Do you see it too?" Hillary says.

"This is our access between the chakras. Let's go in." I say.

We enter the elevator, which takes us up, and as the doors slide open we notice that she is on the orange level.

Hillary feels the intensity shift to her lower abdomen the moment she steps out of the elevator.

"Whoa. That felt strange."

"It's okay, Hillary." I say, "We're here in our bodies, just taking an energetic journey.

Although Hillary can see the walls and floor, she can only feel me next to her. I whisper, "The Anuenue are near and they wish to remove me for my part in destroying the portal."

"But, Moa, you didn't do anyth...." A piercing pain in her lower abdomen cuts off Hillary's words.

The Anuenue man, Paul, who previously escorted Heidi, Molly and Hillary into the thorny brush, materializes. His appearance causes Hillary a great deal of pain. She doubles over, however, I energetically place a hand over the pain. "Your Second chakra is located just below your belly button between your front and back. Send a beam of healing white light and say the word 'VAM,'" I say. "Direct the vibration of your tone and the light into the pain to clear and vibrate any darkness or sluggishness away. Repeat the use of the white light energy until you see and feel your Second chakra spinning clockwise and bright orange. Breathe in secure, calm and centering orange energy. You can do this, Hillary."

Hillary's pain subsides and Paul dematerializes. When she is able to sit up again, she says. "I can see you. How did the Anuenue get here? I thought we were just taking a journey in our own bodies?"

"We are in our own bodies, but on another tuner. Remember when I said moving between the worlds was like a DVR?" I say, "Humans are able to do this by meditation."

An elevator door appears right in front of us. We enter the elevator, and I press the yellow level button.

I feel the intensity shift to my Third chakra the moment we step out of the elevator. Before we enter an empty light-filled room, I stop Hillary, "I may repeat myself, but you must relax and do exactly as I say."

Hillary gives me a reverent nod, as we silently move into the room and sit across from one another on the floor.

"Focus on your Third chakra which is behind your solar plexus. What does it look like? If there are any dark spots on your chakra or it looks or feels like it is unusually large or small, slow or fast, send a beam of healing white light and hear the mantra "RAM" directly into the Third chakra to clear and vibrate any darkness or sluggishness away. Repeat the use of the white light energy until you see and feel your Third chakra spinning clockwise and bright yellow. Breathe in secure, calm and centering yellow energy.

"My chest is vibrating." Hillary says.

"That is the fear releasing. Sometimes we hold fear in different parts of our body and this your own way of letting go of fear."

Once again, the elevator door appears. This time, as we enter, Hillary presses the green level button.

"This is so cool! I can feel a shift of intensity to my Fourth chakra." She says excitedly.

We exit into another open, light-filled room with no furnishings.

Again, I say, "Focus on your Fourth chakra. This is called your 'Heart chakra.' What does it look like? If there are any dark spots on your chakra or it looks or feels like it is unusually large or small, slow or fast, send a beam of healing white light and say the mantra "YAM" as you send the light into your Fourth chakra to clear and vibrate any darkness or sluggishness away. Repeat the use of the white light energy until you see and feel your Fourth chakra spinning clockwise and bright green. Breathe in secure, calm and centering green energy."

The elevator door appears right in front of you, and we travel up to the blue level. This time, as the doors open, Hillary skips out into the light filled room.

"I feel wonderful!" Spinning in circles with her arms outstretched, she yells, "I feel a tickle in my throat."

"That is your Fifth chakra," I say. "The moment you stepped out of the elevator I felt it too."

We both spin a yell, "Wheeee!" all the while laughing and focusing on our Fifth chakra.

"Mine is watery and uneven." Hillary says after we've settled down. "It also has dark spots and feels tiny."

"Send a beam of healing white light and chant the mantra "HAM" directly into the Fifth chakra to clear and vibrate any darkness or sluggishness away." I say. "Repeat the use of the white light energy until you see and feel your Fifth chakra spinning clockwise and bright blue. Breathe in secure, calm and centering blue energy."

"Right on cue." Hillary says. Her eyes are bright and she has more energy than I've ever seen her have.

The elevator door appears and we enter. I hit the indigo button. "The Sixth chakra is also called 'the Third Eye.'" I say.

We step out of the elevator and walk out into a light filled room.

"Your Sixth chakra is located in the middle of your forehead between your eyes. This chakra controls your intuition. If there are any dark spots on your chakra or it looks or feels like it is unusually large or small, slow or fast, send a beam of healing white light and say the mantra "OM" while sending light into the Sixth chakra to clear and vibrate any darkness or sluggishness away. Repeat the use of the white light energy until you see and feel your Sixth chakra spinning clockwise and bright indigo. Breathe in secure, calm and centering indigo energy."

When we are finished, I say, "We have one more level to go." For the final time, the elevator door appears and we enter white level.

"Oh, my head." Hillary says. "I feel dizzy!"

"The intensity you feel is an energetic shift to your Seventh chakra," I say as we step out of the elevator.

"Come lie down here, Hillary." I motion for her to rest on a mat. "We're going to do the same exercise that we did with the other chakras. Focus on your Seventh chakra. It is the center of compassion, cosmic knowledge and enlightenment. What does your seventh chakra look like?"

"It looks hazy," Hillary says slowly. "Oh...it hurts" she lets out a low moan.

"Uh oh. I'd better show you this." I hand Hillary a mirror.

CHAPTER XIII
A New Life

Ritual: Embracing New Adventures
Oil: Base of Almond Oil – Black Pepper,
Frankincense, Fennel
Incense: Lavender
Incantation: "All is well."

*During a new moon, light the lavender and anoint your throat
and back of your neck as well as the base of your spine and
bottom of your feet. Sit in a quiet place where you will remain
uninterrupted. Bring your attention to your heart. Now, imagine
you are walking down a dimly lit hallway and you arrive at a
beautiful, solid door. Release any fear that arises about walking
through the door. Open the door and walk through. What do you
see? What do you feel? When you are finished,
write about your experience.*

It is your choice to move forward. Know that
you are protected as you proceed with joy.

✛

Hillary moans again, for now she sees the cause of her pain—a large Anuenue shadow is sitting on her head. It has long ears, a pointy long nose and its wiry legs and green skin make it look less human and more like a storybook goblin. "Get off," she says weakly to the shadow.

"Let's both send some white light energy to your crown chakra and see if it lifts."

I begin to chant 'OM' directly into her Seventh chakra to clear and vibrate any darkness or sluggishness away. I repeat the use of the white light energy until she begins to regain consciousness.

"Breathe in transcending, divine and angelic white energy," I softly whisper to her. "This will heal and protect your body. You have ascended to the highest place in yourself. Now, lie still and imagine this angelic energy clearing away any last bits of negativity or dark energy out of your body."

Hillary is weak, but conscious and I continue, "Feel it drawing out any discomfort or pain either physical or emotional. Then, imagine the white light filling in the empty places and the darkness. The divine white light energy spills out of your body into your aura and circulates, creating a divine shield of white light."

In spite of our intense efforts, the shadow does not budge. It speaks directly to me. "The only way I'll leave is if you become human."

"No, Moa." Hillary says weakly, "Don't do it."

"Hillary, this is a Hekili Anuenue, if it stays put, the pressure on your brain will slowly shut off every organ in your body. You'll die within the week."

"I will become human if you agree to open the portal fully for all who wish to gain access."

The jubilant Hekili Anuenue extends its arms toward my chest and pulls a golden stream of light energy from me. I slump over, exhausted and drained of my Ancient essence, which I have just given over to the Hekili Anuenue to save Hillary.

"NO!" Hillary screams.

The Anuenue shadow turns into an enormous dark cloud that emerges from the top of Hillary's head. Overcome with terror and pain Hillary slips into deep unconsciousness.

We are both finally able to rest after our arduous energetic journey and return to the confines of the tiny "China Shop" apartment.

The sun streams through the weather-streaked window directly onto Hillary's face. We wake to the sound of the dead bolt turning.

I awaken with a start then remember, with a smile, my choice to be human. "Hillary."

Hillary sits up, blinks and shields her eyes from a blinding sun. A slight movement to the left helps her out of the direct shaft of light from the sole window in the China Shop's back room. "Moa?" She says softly.

The frail man appears at the door, nods to us and walks away leaving the door wide open. "Here." Hillary sits up, pulls a tissue from a box on the low coffee table and presses it over my right temple, amazed and grateful at my tremendous sacrifice. "Looks like you got cut on your way back to earth."

I put my finger up to the cut and examine it closely. The blood is red, sticky and definitely mine. "We made it with two hours to spare." I say proudly.

We rise, then embrace and walk hand in hand back to Molly's house.

The sweet evening breeze brings in feelings: soft flowing excitement, smooth wondrous love and sparkling curiosity. I treasure these emotions like priceless gems. Hillary looks lost in thought.

She smiles and looks over, "You know what?"

My answer surprises us both, "No, what?" For I no longer have the ability to read minds and know what can be known before it reaches the conscious mind.

"I love having you here in flesh and blood." Hillary gives me a warm hug and directs me to a chair in the roomy kitchen.

I am given lau lau and rice and a warm loving reception. Hillary and I fill Molly and Heidi in on the day's extraordinary events.

"I'm so glad you are okay." Molly says as she embraces me.

"Me too!" Heidi takes my hand and looks deeply into my eyes. "You can stay in my room if you want."

Molly smiles "No sweetheart, Moa should have her own room.

She is a kind person and a lovely mother. And after I finish my meal, they all escort me to a beautiful pink and green room at the opposite end of the house from all the other rooms. My windows face an enormous Eucalyptus tree. Molly gives me fresh towels, a new bar of soap, a toothbrush and toothpaste, then, they show me around the house and we end up back in the kitchen.

"If you get up before us in the morning, you can come down here and get yourself some cereal or toast. Now, it's time for

140

bed." Molly puts her hand on my shoulder lovingly then adds as she, Hillary and Heidi walk to their rooms for the night, "Don't forget to brush your teeth."

"I love you, Molly." I'm finding it's rather nice not reading people's thoughts.

Early the next morning, the orange sun peeks from the horizon. The portal is fully open and I can't see, but can feel the difference. It's almost like the park's air has been filtered and as the sun hits the patch of earth where I remember the ancient portal once was, a small sparrow rolls and flutters in the dusty dirt and it is soon joined by three, then five, then ten of the tiny birds. The birds flap and move covering themselves in a dirt bath. I sit in Thomas Square with my knees to my chest weeping.

I hear Hillary's voice first, "There she is!"

By the time I look up and clear the tears from my eyes, I see Molly, Hillary, and Heidi bounding across the street and through the dew-moistened grass. The relief and worry tumbles out all at once in a jumble.

"We looked everywhere!" Hillary reaches me first.

"You weren't in the kitchen and then I looked..." From behind her Heidi chimes in.

"The front door was unlocked so we figured out that you had left." Hillary adds.

"But we were so worried! Oh, Moa." Finally, Molly reaches the group out of breath. "What were you thinking going out without telling us where you were going?"

"I want my mom!" This is the first chance I have had to cry about my loss since losing her all those years ago.

Heidi sits on the wall next to me and puts her arms around me. "I've felt that way before, too. But, I can't imagine what it would be like to never see both parents again."

Hillary and Molly come over and put their hands on my shoulders, their warmth and generosity enveloping me in love.

"With access to the ancient portal finally regained, I feel lost. It was my job for so long." I rest my forehead on my knees and Hillary places a hand on my back and gives it a few gentle pats.

Heidi pulls her mother aside and says something I can't hear. When they return, Molly speaks first, "Moa, we would love it if you would come and live with us."

"I'd love to." I smile and give them each a hug.

The sparrows continue to shake the dust through their wings staying within the confines of an invisible circle. I am thankful that all souls are free to move through the portal from now on.

We return to the house—our house—for a filling breakfast of pancakes, bacon and eggs. Molly makes a smiley face out of my pancake—very clever!

After breakfast, we go to the beach.

The sand is warm and cozy on my feet, and the water... well, the water is glorious. The cool clear salty waves splash around my legs and Heidi and I run back and forth with the waves. Heidi shows me how she builds a drip sand castle and, although it has been a long time, I explain my sand molding technique.

Heidi tells me about school and summer vacation and I tell her about the history of the Hawaiian Islands.

We hike up Diamond Head marveling at the city below. It seems much different being grounded on the earth. I watch a Hawaiian hawk swoop and soar above. Only a few days ago I was up with that hawk.

"Diamond Head is a volcanic crater which has been extinct for 150,000 years." I say.

"Wow, Moa." Hillary laughs, "That's even older than you are."

"There aren't a lot of things you can say that about," I laugh, too.

"Keep going," Molly says, "I want to know more about Diamond Head. You are a walking encyclopedia!"

"Its original name, Laeahi," I continue, "means 'brow of the tuna' because its peak looks like a tuna head from afar, but the name was changed when, in the 1800s, British sailors first saw stones glistening in the soil and thought the crater contained diamonds."

"Does it?" Heidi says excitedly.

"No. It's just calcite." I say.

"So, Moa. Now that you're human, how will you protect yourself?" Hillary asks.

"I know I can access my own chi energy or Peko energy, which allows me to create protection. I remember everything, so at least I still have that power. But I can no longer move between the worlds or change form."

We head down in silence. Then, I look out over Waikiki Beach. "This island has seen so much," I say.

"So have you," Hillary says.

That night, I am awakened from a dream. In it, I was back on the island with my first family. My mother gave me a beautifully fragrant floral pikake lei and told me I had completed the first part of my journey and now must heal the earth.

I run down the hall to Hillary's room and climb into bed with her. When I didn't have form, I forgot how comforting it could feel to have a warm human body to snuggle up against. There, I fall peacefully back to sleep.

I'm the last to rise the next morning. When I wander downstairs the three greet me warmly. The smell of brewed coffee and freshly squeezed orange juice draws me to the table. A small television sits on the counter. The news is on, the sound muted.

"How'd you sleep?" Hillary says.

"I dreamt I was back home with my old family. My mother gave me a lei and told me about the next leg of my journey."

"What was your mother like?" Heidi has grabbed Hillary's colorful sunglasses from the countertop and puts them on.

"She was a kind woman—soft-spoken. Fabric making was her gift to the world. But my sisters and I loved her ability to weave stories. My father was a superb storyteller, but my mother was able to draw anyone who was listening into the story and make them feel like they had been on the adventure, too." I smile, imagining her bending over her work, talking joyously of her youth.

"Hey, the Anuenue are on TV!" Heidi stares at the television, the glasses perched upon her nose almost swallow her face whole.

Molly grabs the remote and turns up the volume.

"Two teens have been arrested in Honolulu in connection with the thefts of three priceless Egyptian museum pieces and are awaiting extradition to Cairo. They are members of a group called the "Rindodala" sect and they have accepted responsibility for the thefts."

"That's my mother's statue!" I yell.

The camera follows the two boys. One is tall with long dark hair, the other is short and stocky with a buzz haircut. Next, the announcer details the stolen loot and I point to a delicate black six-inch tall statue inlaid with precious pink coral that used to sit in our home.

"That one! My mother received it for her hard work weaving cloth." I bellow.

Both are being led away in handcuffs and the shorter of the two looks into a camera and says, "It is time for our ancient treasures to come home!" Then, a tall, dark haired male Guardian steps between the young man and the camera and says, "The boys will be taken into custody by their father Emel Shanheer, a blood descendant of King Tutankhamen."

Without the glasses, everyone looks the same. However, when we borrow the glasses, we finally see who Heidi means.

"There!" Heidi points.

The taller boy is dressed in an Anuenue shirt!

A chorus of astonished responses follows as Molly flips off the television.

"How is that possible?" Hillary gapes.

"This means there are more all over the world." I hop off my chair and start to run out the door, but Hillary catches me.

"Where are you going?" Hillary says.

"I'm going to get my mother's statue back." I say. "Now that I'm human, I can finally hold it in my hands. If I can do that, I may be able to reconnect with her spirit just like Molly and Heidi did with Steve in the angelic realm."

"Wait," Hillary says, "I'll go with you."

We walk to the courthouse through the beautiful moist morning air. The sharply floral scent of star jasmine lingers.

"It smells like an adventure." Moa says as we cross the street toward City Hall. We locate a standing display map of all the surrounding departmental buildings including the County Courthouse.

The boys are in the County jail. At least that is what the woman at the Courthouse tells us and, she adds matter-of-factly, they are not allowed visitors.

"I don't care," I say as we exit the courthouse into the searing sun, "The Statue of Ku is staying here with me or in Hawaii."

"Excuse me." We turn to see the Guardian from TV! He is wearing an Aloha shirt with khaki shorts and looks at me in most patronizing manner. "I didn't know the locals cared this much about the simple pilfering of a few artifacts."

"Sir," I say. "One of the statues is mine."

"I'm afraid all of the artifacts are unattainable." The Guardian's says brusquely.

Furious at being given the brush off, I use an equally strong tone, "Where is it?"

"Dear, you seem quite upset about your loss, but you must go through certain channels." The Guardian takes a step toward a waiting limousine. Then his tone becomes a little gentler, "Perhaps you could ask your mother to help you..."

Tears well up in my eyes. I clench my fists and upon seeing my reaction, Hillary puts her arms around my shoulders.

"The artifacts are already in Egypt." The Guardian yells behind him. "Much too far away." Then he strides toward a white, stretch limousine parked on the street. A beefy driver dressed in navy suit opens the door and the Guardian stops to speak with him.

Without a thought, I run toward the open door and jump in the elegant car.

"Moa!" Hillary screams, running behind me. She jumps into the long back seat.

"Get out!" The driver pulls on Hillary's shirt trying to extract her from the roomy limo.

Hillary in-turn grabs me and after a great effort, the driver manages to lug us out. We tumble onto the curb.

"Look, Sir" Hillary manages to pull us both up as she straightens her shirt and pleads with the Guardian. "My friend's mother has died and she merely wants to get back a precious heirloom, the Statue of Ku. You can understand that, can't you?"

This seems to touch a chord with the Guardian and he softens. We wait tensely while he grapples with some unknown mysterious internal battle. "Okay. I'll make a deal with you. You may come to Egypt on the prince's private jet and stay at our expense if the Statue of Ku is indeed your mother's heirloom. If, however, it is proven that the Statue of Ku is not your mother's, you will both be jailed and forced to find your own way home as well as covering all expenses incurred on this trip."

Without a second thought I grab Hillary's hand and, this time, we slip back into the limousine, the Guardian follows us and shuts the door firmly.

A worried look covers Hillary's face, "We need to tell Molly where we're going." She digs through her ample purse to pull out her cell phone and catches the glint of the opalescent stone she picked up on her first day in Thomas

Square Park and holds it up to the light. "Hi Molly," the sparkling stone throws tiny light-rainbows over Hillary and I, "you're never going to believe this..."

Before she finishes, I grab the phone, "We're going to Egypt!" I yell into the phone as the Honolulu hubbub zips past and we speed toward Honolulu International Airport and the Statue of Ku.

Dreading an airplane ride, Hillary blurts, "Oh, Moa. We're not prepared. We don't know these people! What if they hurt us? You're mortal and I'm...well, I don't know what I'm doing. Oh, no. The wicked are sure to win."

I look deeply into Hillary's moist eyes. "Don't you know? Evil only shows up to prove that good exists. There is no way evil can win."

End

Discover other books in the Moa Series:
<u>Statue of Ku</u>
<u>The Iron Shinto</u>

About the Author

Tricia Stewart Shiu is an award-winning screenwriter, author and playwright, but her passion lies in creating mystical stories. Her latest series, The Moa Books, which includes Moa, The Statue of Ku and The Iron Shinto were by far, her favorite to write.

Learn More about Moa
Facebook:
http://www.facebook.com/MoaBook
Website:
http://www.Moa-Book.com
Moa Blog:
http://tstewartshiu.wordpress.com
Follow Tricia Stewart Shiu on Twitter:
@tstewartshiu

Made in the USA
San Bernardino, CA
23 May 2015